"I won't sleep with you to pay that debt."

Michelle's face was pale as she faced him, her hands twisted together in a tight knot. "Did you come here tonight expecting to whisk me straight up to bed?"

He eyed her sharply. "The thought had crossed my mind. I was willing."

"Well, I'm not!" She tried to control the outrage that burned in her at the insult. She had to control it; she couldn't afford to fall apart now.

"I'm glad, because I've changed my mind." He paused, and the way he was looking at her made her shiver. Then he spoke again, and the image his rough words provoked shot through her brain like lightning. "You'll go to bed with me, all right, but it won't be because of any money you owe me. When the time comes, it will be because you want me just the way I want you."

Dear Reader,

When two people fall in love, the world is suddenly new and exciting, and it's that same excitement we bring to you in Silhouette Intimate Moments. These are stories with scope, with grandeur. The characters lead the lives we all dream of, and everything they do reflects the wonder of being in love.

Longer and more sensuous than most romances, Silhouette Intimate Moments novels take you away from everyday life and let you share the magic of love. Adventure, glamour, drama, even suspense—these are the passwords that let you into a world where love has a power beyond the ordinary, where the best authors in the field today create stories of love and commitment that will stay with you always.

In coming months look for novels by your favorite authors: Maura Seger, Parris Afton Bonds, Linda Howard, and Nora Roberts, to name just a few. And whenever you buy books, look for all the Silhouette Intimate Moments, love stories *for* today's women *by* today's women.

Leslie J. Wainger
Senior Editor
Silhouette Books

Linda Howard
Heartbreaker

Silhouette Intimate Moments

Published by Silhouette Books New York

America's Publisher of Contemporary Romance

Books by Linda Howard

Silhouette Special Edition

All That Glitters #22
An Independent Wife #46
Come Lie With Me #177
Sarah's Child #230
The Cutting Edge #260
Almost Forever #327

Silhouette Intimate Moments

Against the Rules #22
Tears of the Renegade #92
Midnight Rainbow #129
Diamond Bay #177
Heartbreaker #201

LINDA HOWARD

has been writing books almost as long as she has been reading them. Books, in any form, are the ruling passion of her life, and she cut her teeth on the likes of Margaret Mitchell. She eventually gave up reading anything but romances, since, she says, murder and mayhem and politics bore her. She began writing at the age of nine, but it was only after twenty-one years that she decided to send a book to a publisher. Not surprisingly, it was accepted, and she's never looked back. She lives with her husband in Alabama and is now a veteran of writers' conventions, autograph sessions and award ceremonies.

Chapter 1

She found the paper while she was sorting through the personal things in her father's desk. Michelle Cabot unfolded the single sheet with casual curiosity, just as she had unfolded dozens of others, but she had read only a paragraph when her spine slowly straightened and a tremor began in her fingers. Stunned, she began again, her eyes widening with sick horror at what she read.

Anybody but him. Dear God, anybody but him!

She owed John Rafferty one hundred thousand dollars.

Plus interest, of course. At what percent? She couldn't read any further to find out; instead she dropped the paper onto the littered surface of the desk and sank back in her father's battered old leather chair, her eyes closing against the nausea caused by shock, dread and the particularly sickening feeling of dying hope. She had already been on her knees; this unsuspected debt had smashed her flat.

Why did it have to be John Rafferty? Why not some impersonal bank? The end result would be the same, of course, but the humiliation would be absent. The thought of facing him made her shrivel deep inside, where she protected the tender part of herself. If Rafferty ever even suspected that that tenderness existed, she was lost. A dead duck...or a sitting one, if it made any difference. A gone goose. A cooked goose. Whatever simile she used, it fit.

Her hands were still shaking when she picked up the paper to read it again and work out the details of the financial agreement. John Rafferty had made a personal loan of one hundred thousand dollars to her father, Langley Cabot, at an interest rate two percent lower than the market rate...and the loan had been due four months ago. She felt even sicker. She knew it hadn't been repaid, because she'd gone over every detail of her father's books in an effort to salvage something from the financial disaster he'd been floundering in when he'd died. She had ruthlessly liquidated almost everything to pay the outstanding debts, everything except this ranch, which had been her father's dream and had somehow come to represent a refuge to her. She hadn't liked Florida ten years ago, when her father had sold their home and moved her from their well-ordered, monied existence in Connecticut to the heat and humidity of a cattle ranch in central Florida, but that had been a decade ago, and things changed. People changed, time changed...and time changed people. The ranch didn't represent love or a dream to her; it was, simply, all she had left. Life had seemed so complicated once, but it was remarkable how simple things were when it came down to a matter of survival.

Even now it was hard to just give up and let the inevitable happen. She had known from the beginning that it would be almost impossible for her to keep the ranch and put it back on a paying basis, but she'd been driven to at least *try*. She wouldn't have been able to live with herself if she'd taken the easy way out and let the ranch go.

Now she would have to sell the ranch after all, or at least the cattle; there was no other way she could repay that hundred thousand dollars. The wonder was that Rafferty hadn't already demanded repayment. But if she sold the cattle, what good was the ranch? She'd been depending on the cattle sales to keep her going, and without that income she'd have to sell the ranch anyway.

It was so hard to think of letting the ranch go; she had almost begun to hope that she might be able to hold on to it. She'd been afraid to hope, had tried not to, but still, that little glimmer of optimism had begun growing. Now she'd failed at this, just as she'd failed at everything else in her life: as daughter, wife, and now rancher. Even if Rafferty gave her an extension on the loan, something she didn't expect to happen, she had no real expectation of being able to pay it off when it came due again. The naked truth was that she had no expectations at all; she was merely hanging on.

Well, she wouldn't gain anything by putting it off. She had to talk to Rafferty, so it might as well be now. The clock on the wall said it wasn't quite nine-thirty; Rafferty would still be up. She looked up his number and dialed it, and the usual reaction set in. Even before the first ring sounded, her fingers were locked so tightly around the receiver that her knuckles were white, and her heart had lurched into a fast, heavy pounding that made her feel as if she'd been running. Tension knotted her stomach. Oh, damn! She wouldn't even be able to talk coherently if she didn't get a grip on herself!

The telephone was answered on the sixth ring, and by then Michelle had braced herself for the ordeal of talking to him. When the housekeeper said, "Rafferty residence," Michelle's voice was perfectly cool and even when she asked to speak to Rafferty.

"I'm sorry, he isn't in. May I take a message?"

It was almost like a reprieve, if it hadn't been for the knowledge that now she'd have to do it all over again. "Please have him call Michelle Cabot," she said, and gave the housekeeper her number. Then she asked, "Do you expect him back soon?"

There was only a slight hesitation before the housekeeper said, "No, I think he'll be quite late, but I'll give him your message first thing in the morning."

"Thank you," Michelle murmured, and hung up. She should have expected him to be out. Rafferty was famous, or perhaps notorious was a better word, for his sexual appetite and escapades. If he'd quieted down over the years, it was only in his hell-raising. According to the gossip she'd heard from time to time, his libido was alive and well; a look from those hard, dark eyes still made a woman's pulse go wild, and he looked at a lot of women, but Michelle wasn't one of them. Hostility had exploded between them at their first meeting, ten years before, and at best their relationship was an armed standoff. Her father had been a buffer between them, but now he was dead, and she expected the worst. Rafferty didn't do things by half measures.

There was nothing she could do about the loan that night, and she'd lost her taste for sorting through the remainder of her father's papers, so she decided to turn in. She took a quick shower; her sore muscles would have liked a longer one, but she was doing everything she could to keep her electricity bill down, and since she got her water from a well, and the water was pumped by an electric pump, small luxuries had to go to make way for the more important ones, like eating.

But as tired as she was, when she was lying in bed she couldn't go to sleep. The thought of talking to Rafferty filled her mind again, and once more her heartbeat speeded up. She tried to take deep, slow breaths. It had always been like this, and it was even worse when she had to see him face to face. If only he wasn't so big! But he was six feet three inches and about two hundred pounds of muscled masculinity; he was good at dwarfing other people. Whenever he was close, Michelle felt threatened in some basic way, and even thinking of him made her feel suffocated. No other man in the world made her react the way he did; no one else could make her so angry, so wary—or so excited in a strange, primitive way.

It had been that way from the beginning, from the moment she'd met him ten years before. She had been eighteen then, as spoiled as he'd accused her of being, and as haughty as only a teenager standing on her dignity could be. His reputation had preceded him, and Michelle had been determined to show him that *she* couldn't be lumped with all the women who panted after him. As if he would have been interested in a teenager! she thought wryly, twisting on the bed in search of comfort. What a child she'd been! A silly, spoiled, frightened child.

Because John Rafferty *had* frightened her, even though he'd all but ignored her. Or rather, her own reaction had frightened her. He'd been twenty-six, a *man*, as opposed to the boys she was used to, and a man who had already turned a smallish central Florida cattle ranch into a growing, thriving empire by his own force of will and years of backbreaking work. Her first sight of him, towering over her father while the two men talked cattle, had scared her half to death. Even now she could recall her sudden breathlessness, as if she'd been punched in the stomach.

They'd been standing beside Rafferty's horse, and he'd had one arm draped across the saddle while his other hand was propped negligently on his hip. He'd been six feet and three inches of sheer power, all hard muscle and intensity, dominating even the big animal with his will. She'd already heard about him; men laughed and called him a "stud" in admiring tones, and women called him the same thing, but always in excited, half-fearful whispers. A woman might be given the benefit of the doubt after going out with him once, but if she went out with him twice it was accepted that she had been to bed with him. At the time Michelle hadn't even considered that his reputation was probably exaggerated. Now that she was older, she still didn't consider it. There was just something about the way Rafferty looked that made a woman believe all the tales about him.

But even his reputation hadn't prepared her for the real man, for the force and energy that radiated from him. Life burned hotter and brighter in some people, and John Rafferty was one of them. He was a dark fire, dominating his surroundings with his height and powerful build, dominating people with his forceful, even ruthless, personality.

Michelle had sucked in her breath at the sight of him, the sun glinting off his coal-black hair, his dark eyes narrowed under prominent black brows, a neat black mustache shadowing the firm line of his upper lip. He'd been darkly tanned, as he always was from hours of working outside in all seasons; even as she'd watched, a trickle of sweat had run down his temple to curve over his high, bronzed cheekbone before tacking down his cheek to finally drip off his square jaw. Patches of sweat had darkened his blue work shirt under his arms and on his chest and back. But even sweat and dirt couldn't detract from the aura of a powerful, intensely sexual male animal; perhaps they had even added to it. The hand on his hip had drawn her gaze downward to his hips and long legs, and the faded tight jeans had outlined his body so faithfully that her mouth had gone dry. Her heart had stopped beating for a moment, then lurched into a heavy rhythm that made her entire body throb. She'd been eighteen, too young to handle what she felt, too young to handle the man, and her own reaction had frightened her. Because of that, she'd been at her snooty best when she'd walked up to her father to be introduced.

They'd gotten off on the wrong foot and had been there ever since. She was probably the only woman in the world at odds with Rafferty, and she wasn't certain, even now, that she wanted it to be any different. Somehow she felt safer knowing that he disliked her; at least he wouldn't be turning that formidable charm of his on her. In that respect, hostility brought with it a certain amount of protection.

A shiver ran over her body as she lay in bed thinking about both him and what she'd admitted only to herself: she was no more immune to Rafferty than the legion of women who had already succumbed. She was safe only as long as he didn't realize how vulnerable she was to his potent masculinity. He would delight in taking advantage of his power over her, making her pay for all the cutting remarks she'd made to him over the years, and for all the other things he disliked about her. To protect herself, she had to hold him at bay with hostility; it was rather ironic that now she needed his goodwill in order to survive financially.

She had almost forgotten how to laugh except for the social sounds that passed for laughter but held no humor, or how to smile except for the false mask of cheerfulness that kept pity away, but in the darkness and privacy of her bedroom she felt a wry grin curving her mouth. If she had to depend on Rafferty's goodwill for survival, she might as well go out to the pasture, dig a hole and pull the dirt in over herself to save him the time and trouble.

The next morning she loitered around the house waiting for him to call for as long as she could, but she had chores to do, and the cattle wouldn't wait. Finally she gave up and trudged out to the barn, her mind already absorbed with the hundred and one problems the ranch presented every day. She had several fields of hay that needed to be cut and baled, but she'd been forced to sell the tractor and hay baler; the only way she could get the hay cut would be to offer someone part of the hay if they'd do the cutting and baling for her. She backed the pickup truck into the barn and climbed into the hayloft, counting the bales she had left. The supply was dwindling; she'd have to do something soon.

There was no way she could lift the heavy bales, but she'd developed her own system for handling them. She had parked the truck just under the door to the hayloft, so all she had to do was push the bales to the open door and tip them through to land in the truck bed. Pushing the hay wasn't easy; they were supposed to be hundred-pound bales, which meant that she outweighed them by maybe seventeen pounds...if she hadn't lost weight, which she suspected she had, and if the bales weighed only a hundred pounds, which she suspected they didn't. Their weight varied, but some of them were so heavy she could barely move them an inch at a time.

She drove the truck across the pasture to where the cattle grazed; heads lifted, dark brown eyes surveyed the familiar truck, and the entire herd began ambling toward her. Michelle stopped the truck and climbed in back. Tossing the bales out was impossible, so she cut the twine there in the back of the truck and loosened the hay with the pitchfork she had brought along, then pitched the hay out in big clumps. She got back in the truck, drove a piece down the pasture, and stopped to repeat the procedure. She did it until the back of the pickup was empty, and by the time she was finished her shoulders were aching so badly the muscles felt as if they were on fire. If the herd hadn't been badly diminished in numbers from what it had been, she couldn't have handled it. But if the herd were larger, she reminded herself, she'd be able to afford help. When she remembered the number of people who used to work on the ranch, the number needed to keep it going properly, a wave of hopelessness hit her. Logic told her there was no way she could do it all herself.

But what did logic have to do with cold reality? She had to do it herself because she had no one else. Sometimes she thought that was the one thing life seemed determined to teach her: that she could depend only on herself, that there was no one she could trust, no one she could rely on, no one strong enough to stand behind her and hold her up when she needed to rest. There had been times when she'd felt a crushing sense of loneliness, especially since her father had died, but there was also a certain perverse comfort in knowing she could rely on no one but herself. She expected nothing of other people, therefore she wasn't disappointed by any failure on their part to live up to her expectations. She simply accepted facts as they were, without any pretty dressing up, did what she had to do, and went on from there. At least she was free now, and no longer dreaded waking up each day.

She trudged around the ranch doing the chores, putting her mind in neutral gear and simply letting her body go through the motions. It was easier that way; she could pay attention to her aches and bruises when all the chores were finished, but the best way to get them done was to ignore the protests of her muscles and the nicks and bruises she acquired. None of her old friends would ever have believed that Michelle Cabot was capable of turning her dainty hands to rough, physical chores. Sometimes it amused her to imagine what their reactions would be, another mind game that she played with herself to pass the time. Michelle Cabot had always been ready for a party, or shopping, or a trip to St. Moritz, or a cruise on someone's yacht. Michelle Cabot had always been laughing, making wisecracks with the best of them; she'd looked perfectly *right* with a glass of champagne in her hand and diamonds in her ears. The ultimate Golden Girl, that was her.

Well, the ultimate Golden Girl had cattle to feed, hay to cut, fences that needed repair, and that was only the tip of the iceberg. She needed to dip the cattle, but that was something else she hadn't figured out how to manage by herself. There was branding, castrating, breeding.... When she allowed herself to think of everything that needed doing, she was swamped by hopelessness, so she usually didn't dwell on it. She just took each day as it came, slogging along, doing what she could. It was survival, and she'd become good at it.

By ten o'clock that night, when Rafferty hadn't called, Michelle braced herself and called him again. Again the housekeeper answered; Michelle stifled a sigh, wondering if Rafferty ever spent a night at home. "This is Michelle Cabot. I'd like to speak to Rafferty, please. Is he home?"

"Yes, he's down at the barn. I'll switch your call to him."

So he had a telephone in the barn. For a moment she thought enviously of the operation he had as she listened to the clicks the receiver made in her ear. Thinking about his ranch took her mind off her suddenly galloping pulse and stifled breathing.

"Rafferty." His deep, impatient voice barked the word in her ear, and she jumped, her hand tightening on the receiver as her eyes closed.

"This is Michelle Cabot." She kept her tone as remote as possible as she identified herself. "I'd like to talk to you, if you have the time."

"Right now I'm damned short of time. I've got a mare in foal, so spit it out and make it fast."

"It'll take more time than that. I'd like to make an appointment, then. Would it be convenient for me to come over tomorrow morning?"

He laughed, a short, humorless bark. "This is a working ranch, sugar, not a social event. I don't have time for you tomorrow morning. Time's up."

"Then when?"

He muttered an impatient curse. "Look, I don't have time for you *now*. I'll drop by tomorrow afternoon on my way to town. About six." He hung up before she could agree or disagree, but as she hung up, too, she thought ruefully that he was calling the shots, so it didn't really matter if she liked the time or not. At least she had the telephone call behind her now, and there were almost twenty hours in which to brace herself for actually seeing him. She would stop work tomorrow in time to shower and wash her hair, and she'd do the whole routine with makeup and perfume, wear her white linen trousers and white silk shirt. Looking at her, Rafferty would never suspect that she was anything other than what he'd always thought her to be, pampered and useless.

It was late in the afternoon, the broiling sun had pushed the temperature to a hundred degrees, and the cattle were skittish. Rafferty was hot, sweaty, dusty and ill-tempered, and so were his men. They'd spent too much time chasing after strays instead of getting the branding and inoculating done, and now the deep, threatening rumble of thunder signaled a summer thunderstorm. The men speeded up their work, wanting to get finished before the storm hit.

Dust rose in the air as the anxious bawling increased in volume and the stench of burning hide intensified. Rafferty worked with the men, not disdaining any of the dirty jobs. It was *his* ranch, his life. Ranching was hard, dirty work, but he'd made it profitable when others had gone under, and he'd done it with his own sweat and steely determination. His mother had left rather than tolerate the life; of course, the ranch had been much smaller back then, not like the empire he'd built. His father, and the ranch, hadn't been able to support her in the style she'd wanted. Rafferty sometimes got a grim satisfaction from the knowledge that now his mother regretted having been so hasty to desert her husband and son so long ago. He didn't hate her; he didn't waste that much effort on her. He just didn't have much use for her, or for any of the rich, spoiled, bored, *useless* people she considered her friends.

Nev Luther straightened from the last calf, wiping his sweaty face on his shirt sleeve, then glancing at the sun and the soaring black cloud bank of the approaching storm. "Well, that's it," he grunted. "We'd better get loaded up before that thing hits." Then he glanced at his boss. "Ain't you supposed to see that Cabot gal today?"

Nev had been in the barn with Rafferty when he'd talked to Michelle, so he'd overheard the conversation. After a quick look at his watch, Rafferty swore aloud. He'd forgotten about her, and he wasn't grateful to Nev for reminding him. There were few people walking the earth who irritated him as much as Michelle Cabot.

"Damn it, I guess I'd better go," he said reluctantly. He knew what she wanted. It had surprised him that she had called at all, rather than continuing to ignore the debt. She was probably going to whine about how little money she had left and tell him that she couldn't *possibly* scrape up that amount. Just thinking about her made him want to grab her and shake her, hard. Or better yet, take a belt to her backside. She was exactly what he disliked most: a spoiled, selfish parasite who'd never done a day's work in her life. Her father had bankrupted himself paying for her pleasure jaunts, but Langley Cabot had always been a bit of a fool where his beloved only child had been concerned. Nothing had been too good for darling little Michelle, nothing at all.

Too bad that darling Michelle was a spoiled brat. Damn, she irritated him! She'd irritated him from the first moment he'd seen her, prissing up to where her father had stood talking to him, with her haughty nose in the air as if she'd smelled something bad. Well, maybe she had. Sweat, the product of physical work, was an alien odor to her. She'd looked at him the way she would have looked at a worm, then dismissed him as unimportant and turned her back to him while she coaxed and wheedled something out of her father with that charming Golden Girl act of hers.

"Say, boss, if you don't want to see that fancy little thing, I'd be happy to fill in for you," Nev offered, grinning.

"It's tempting," Rafferty said sourly, checking his watch again. He could go home and clean up, but it would make him late. He wasn't that far from the

Cabot ranch now, and he wasn't in the mood to drive all the way back to his house, shower, and then make the drive again just so he wouldn't offend her dainty nose. She could put up with him as he was, dirt, sweat and all; after all, she was the one begging for favors. The mood he was in, he just might call in that debt, knowing good and well she couldn't pay it. He wondered with sardonic amusement if she would offer to pay it in another way. It would serve her right if he played along; it would make her squirm with distaste to think of letting him have her pampered body. After all, he was rough and dirty and worked for a living.

As he strode over to his truck and slid his long length under the steering wheel, he couldn't keep the image from forming in his mind: the image of Michelle Cabot lying beneath him, her slim body naked, her pale gold hair spread out over his pillow as he moved in and out of her. He felt his loins become heavy and full in response to the provocative image, and he swore under his breath. Damn her, and damn himself. He'd spent years watching her, brooding, wanting her and at the same time wanting to teach her in whatever way it took not to be such a spoiled, selfish snob.

Other people hadn't seen her that way; she could be charming when she chose, and she'd chosen to work that charm on the local people, maybe just to amuse herself with their gullibility. The ranchers and farmers in the area were a friendly group, rewarding themselves for their endless hard work with informal get-togethers, parties and barbecues almost every weekend, and Michelle had had them all eating out of her hand. They didn't see the side of her that she'd revealed to him; she was always laughing, dancing...but never with him. She would dance with every other man there, but never with him. He'd watched her, all right, and because he was a healthy male with a healthy libido he hadn't been able to stop himself from responding physically to her lithe, curved body and sparkling smile, even though it made him angry that he responded to her in any way. He didn't want to want her, but just looking at her made him hungry.

Other men had watched her with hungry eyes, too, including Mike Webster. Rafferty didn't think he'd ever forgive her for what she'd done to Mike, whose marriage had been shaky even before Michelle had burst onto the scene with her flirtatious manner and sparkling laughter. Mike hadn't been any match for her; he'd fallen hard and fast, and the Webster marriage had splintered beyond repair. Then Michelle had flitted on to fresher prey, and Mike had been left with nothing but a ruined life. The young rancher had lost everything he'd worked for, forced to sell his ranch because of the divorce settlement. He was just one more man Michelle had ruined with her selfishness, as she'd ruined her father. Even when Langley was deep in financial trouble he'd kept providing money for Michelle's expensive life-style. Her father had been going under, but she'd still insisted on buying her silks and jewels, and skiing vacations in St. Moritz. It would take a rich man to afford Michelle Cabot, and a strong one.

The thought of being the one who provided her with those things, and the one who had certain rights over her because of it, teased his mind with disturbing persistence. No matter how angry, irritated or disgusted he felt toward her, he couldn't control his physical response to her. There was something about her that made him want to reach out and take her. She looked, sounded and smelled expensive; he wanted to know if she tasted expensive, too, if her skin was as silky as it looked. He wanted to bury his hands in her sunlit hair, taste her wide, soft mouth, and trace his fingertips across the chiseled perfection of her cheekbones, inhale the gut-tightening fragrance of her skin. He'd smelled her the day they'd first met, the perfume in her hair and on her skin, and the sweetness of her flesh beneath it. She was expensive all right, too expensive for Mike Webster, and for the poor sap she'd married and then left, certainly too expensive for her father. Rafferty wanted to lose himself in all that richness. It was a pure, primitive male instinct, the reaction of the male to a ready female. Maybe Michelle was a tease, but she gave out all the right signals to bring the men running, like bees to the sweetest flower.

Right now Michelle was between supporters, but he knew it wouldn't be long before she had another man lined up. Why shouldn't he be that man? He was tired of wanting her and watching her turn her snooty little nose up at him. She wouldn't be able to wrap him around her finger as she was used to doing, but that would be the price she had to pay for her expensive tastes. Rafferty narrowed his eyes against the rain that began to splat against the windshield, thinking about the satisfaction of having Michelle dependent on him for everything she ate and wore. It was a hard, primitive satisfaction. He would use her to satisfy his burning physical hunger for her, but he wouldn't let her get close enough to cloud his mind and judgment.

He'd never paid for a woman before, never been a sugar daddy, but if that was what it took to get Michelle Cabot, he'd do it. He'd never wanted another woman the way he wanted her, so he guessed it evened out.

The threatening storm suddenly broke, sending a sheet of rain sluicing down the windshield to obscure his vision despite the wipers' best efforts. Gusts of wind shoved at the truck, making him fight to hold it steady on the road. Visibility was so bad that he almost missed the turn to the Cabot ranch even though he knew these roads as well as he knew his own face. His features were dark with ill-temper when he drove up to the Cabot house, and his disgust increased as he looked around. Even through the rain, he could tell the place had gone to hell. The yard was full of weeds, the barn and stables had the forlorn look of emptiness and neglect, and the pastures that had once been dotted with prime Brahman cattle were empty now. The little society queen's kingdom had dissolved around her.

Though he'd pulled the truck up close to the house, it was raining so hard that he was drenched to the skin by the time he sprinted to the porch. He slapped his straw hat against his leg to get most of the water off it, but didn't replace it on his head. He raised his hand to knock, but the door opened before he had a chance. Michelle stood there looking at him with the familiar disdain in her cool, green eyes. She hesitated for just a moment, as if reluctant to let him drip water on the carpet; then she pushed the screen door open and said, ''Come in.'' He imagined it ate at her guts to have to be nice to him because she owed him a hundred thousand dollars.

He walked past her, noting the way she moved back so he wouldn't brush against her. Just wait, he thought savagely. Soon he'd do more than just *brush* against her, and he'd make damned certain she liked it. She might turn her nose up at him now, but things would be different when she was naked under him, her legs wrapped around his waist while she writhed in ecstasy. He didn't just want the use of her body; he wanted her to want him in return, to feel as hungry and obsessed as he did. It would be poetic justice, after all the men she'd used. He almost wanted her to say something snide, so he'd have a reason to put his hands on her, even in anger. He wanted to touch her, no matter what the reason; he wanted to feel her warm and soft in his hands; he wanted to make her respond to him.

But she didn't cut at him with her tongue as she usually did. Instead she said, "Let's go into Dad's office," and led the way down the hall with her perfume drifting behind her to tease him. She looked untouchable in crisp white slacks and a white silk shirt that flowed lovingly over her curvy form, but he itched to touch her anyway. Her sunny pale-gold hair was pulled back and held at the nape of her neck with a wide gold clip.

Her fastidious perfection was in direct contrast to his own rough appearance, and he wondered what she'd do if he touched her, if he pulled her against him and got her silk shirt wet and stained. He was dirty and sweaty and smelled of cattle and horses, and now he was wet into the bargain; no, there was no way she'd accept his touch.

"Please sit down," she said, waving her hand at one of the leather chairs in the office. "I imagine you know why I called."

His expression became even more sardonic. "I imagine I do."

"I found the loan paper when I was going through Daddy's desk the night before last. I don't want you to think that I'm trying to weasel out of paying it, but I don't have the money right now—"

"Don't waste my time," he advised, interrupting.

She stared up at him. He hadn't taken the chair she'd offered; he was standing too close, towering over her, and the look in his black eyes made her shiver.

"What?"

"This song and dance; don't waste my time doing the whole bit. I know what you're going to offer, and I'm willing. I've been wanting to get in your pants for a long time, honey; just don't make the mistake of thinking a few quickies will make us even, because they won't. I believe in getting my money's worth."

Chapter 2

Shock froze her in place and leeched the color from her upturned face until it was as pale as ivory. She felt disoriented; for a moment his words refused to make sense, rotating in her mind like so many unconnected pieces of a puzzle. He was looming over her, his height and muscularity making her feel as insignificant as always, while the heat and scent of his body overwhelmed her senses, confusing her. He was too close! Then the words realigned themselves, and their meaning slapped her in the face. Panic and fury took the place of shock. Without thinking she drew back from him and snapped, "You must be joking!"

It was the wrong thing to say. She knew it as soon as she'd said it. Now wasn't the time to insult him, not when she needed his cooperation if she wanted to have a prayer of keeping the ranch going, but both pride and habit made her lash back at him. She could feel her stomach tighten even as she lifted her chin to give

him a haughty stare, waiting for the reaction that was
sure to come after the inadvertent challenge she'd
thrown in his teeth. It wasn't safe to challenge Rafferty at all, and now she'd done it in the most elemental way possible.

His face was hard and still, his eyes narrowed and
burning as he watched her. Michelle could feel the iron
control he exerted to keep himself from moving. "Do
I look like I'm joking?" he asked in a soft, dangerous
tone. "You've always had some poor sucker support-
ing you; why shouldn't it be my turn? You can't lead
me around by the nose the way you have every other
man, but the way I see it, you can't afford to be too
choosy right now."

"What would *you* know about being choosy?" She
went even whiter, retreating from him a few more
steps; she could almost feel his impact on her skin, and
he hadn't even moved. He'd had so many women that
she didn't even want to think about it, because thinking about it made her hurt deep inside. Had those
other women felt this helpless, this overwhelmed by his
heat and sexuality? She couldn't control her inborn
instincts and responses; she had always sensed her own
weakness where he was concerned, and that was what
frightened her, what had kept her fighting him all
these years. She simply couldn't face being used by
him as casually as a stallion would service a mare; it
would mean too much to her, and too little to him.

"Don't pull away from me," he said, his voice going
even softer, deeper, stroking her senses like dark vel-
vet. It was the voice he would use in the night, she
thought dazedly, her mind filled with the image of him
covering a woman with his lean, powerful body while
he murmured rawly sexual things in her ear. John

wouldn't be a subtle lover; he would be strong and elemental, overwhelming a woman's senses. Wildly she blanked the image from her mind, turning her head away so she couldn't see him.

Rage lashed at him when she turned away as if she couldn't bear the sight of him; she couldn't have made it any plainer that she couldn't bear the idea of sleeping with him, either. With three long strides he circled the desk and caught her upper arms in his lean, sinewy hands, pulling her hard against him. Even in his fury he realized that this was the first time he'd touched her, felt her softness and the fragility of her bones. His hands completely encircled her arms, and his fingers wanted to linger, to stroke. Hunger rose again, pushing aside some of the anger. "Don't turn your nose up at me like some Ice Princess," he ordered roughly. "Your little kingdom has gone to hell, honey, in case you haven't noticed. Those fancy playmates of yours don't know you from Adam's housecat now that you can't afford to play. They sure haven't offered to help, have they?"

Michelle pushed against his chest, but it was like trying to move a wall. "I haven't asked them to help!" she cried, goaded. "I haven't asked anyone for help, least of all *you*!"

"Why not me?" He shook her lightly, his eyes narrowed and fierce. "I can afford you, honey."

"I'm not for sale!" She tried to pull back, but the effort was useless; though he wasn't holding her tightly enough to hurt, she was helpless against his steely strength.

"I'm not interested in buying," he murmured as he dipped his head. "Only in renting you for a while." Michelle made an inarticulate sound of protest and tried to turn her head away, but he simply closed his fist in her hair and held her still for his mouth. Just for a moment she saw his black eyes, burning with hunger, then his mouth was on hers, and she quivered in his arms like a frightened animal. Her eyelashes fluttered shut and she sank against him. For years she'd wondered about his mouth, his taste, if his lips would be firm or soft, if his mustache would scratch. Pleasure exploded in her like a fireball, flooding her with heat. Now she knew. Now she knew the warm, heady taste of his mouth, the firm fullness of his lips, the soft prickle of his mustache, the sure way his tongue moved into her mouth as if it were his right to be so intimate. Somehow her arms were around his shoulders, her nails digging through the wet fabric of his shirt to the hard muscle beneath. Somehow she was arched against him, his arms locked tight as he held her and took her mouth so deeply, over and over again. She didn't feel the moisture from his clothing seeping into hers; she felt only his heat and hardness, and dimly she knew that if she didn't stop soon, *he* wouldn't stop at all.

She didn't want to stop. Already she was coming apart inside, because she wanted nothing more than to simply lie against him and feel his hands on her. She'd known it would be like this, and she'd known she couldn't let it happen, couldn't let him get close to her. The feeling was so powerful that it frightened her. *He* frightened her. He would demand too much from her, take so much that there wouldn't be anything left when he moved on. She'd always known instinctively that she couldn't handle him.

It took every bit of inner strength she had to turn her face away from his mouth, to put her hands on his shoulders and push. She knew she wasn't strong enough to move him; when he released her and moved back a scant few inches, she was bitterly aware that it was by his own choice, not hers. He was watching her, waiting for her decision.

Silence filled the room with a thick presence as she struggled to regain her composure under his unwavering gaze. She could feel the situation slipping out of control. For ten years she had carefully cultivated the hostility between them, terrified of letting him discover that just looking at him turned her bones to water. She'd seen too many of his women with stars in their eyes while he gave them his attention, focusing his intense sexual instincts on them, but all too soon he'd moved on to someone else, and the stars had always turned into hunger and pain and emptiness. Now he was looking at her with that penetrating attention, just what she'd always tried to avoid. She hadn't wanted him to notice her as a woman; she hadn't wanted to join the ranks of all those other women he'd used and left. She had enough trouble now, without adding a broken heart, and John Rafferty was a walking heartache. Her back was already to the wall; she couldn't bear anything else, either emotionally or financially.

But his gaze burned her with black fire, sliding slowly over her body as if measuring her breasts for the way they would fit his hands, her hips for the way his would adjust against them, her legs for the way they would wrap around him in the throes of pleasure. He'd never looked at her in that way before, and it shook her down to her marrow. Pure sexual speculation was in his eyes. In his mind he was already inside her, tasting her, feeling her, giving her pleasure.

It was a look few women could resist, one of un-
ashamed sexuality, carnal experience and an arrogant
confidence that a woman would be ultimately satisfied in his arms. He wanted her; he intended to have
her.

And she couldn't let it happen. She'd been wrapped
in a silken prison her entire life, stifled first by her father's idealistic adoration, then by Roger Beckman's
obsessive jealousy. For the first time in her life she was
alone, responsible for herself and finding some sense
of worth in the responsibility. Fail or succeed, she
needed to do this herself, not run to some man for
help. She looked at John with a blank expression; he
wanted her, but he didn't like or even respect her, and
she wouldn't like or respect herself if she let herself
become the parasite he expected her to be.

Slowly, as if her muscles ached, she eased away
from him and sat down at the desk, tilting her golden
head down so he couldn't see her face. Again, pride
and habit came to her aid; her voice was calm and cool
when she spoke. "As I said, I don't have the money to
repay you right now, and I realize the debt is already
delinquent. The solution depends on you—"

"I've already made my offer," he interrupted, his
eyes narrowing at her coolness. He hitched one hip up
on the desk beside her, his muscled thigh brushing
against her arm. Michelle swallowed to alleviate the
sudden dryness of her mouth, trying not to look at
those powerful, denim-covered muscles. Then he
leaned down, propping his bronzed forearm on his
thigh, and that was worse, because it brought his torso
closer, forcing her to lean back in the chair. "All you
have to do is go ahead and accept it, instead of wast-

ing time pretending you didn't like it when I touched you."

Michelle continued doggedly. "If you want repayment immediately, I'll have to sell the cattle to raise the money, and I'd like to avoid that. I'm counting on the sale of the cattle to keep the ranch going. What I have in mind is to sell some of the land to raise the money, but of course that will take longer. I can't even promise to have the money in six months; it just depends on how fast I can find a buyer." She held her breath, waiting for his response. Selling part of the land was the only plan she'd been able to devise, but it all depended on his cooperation.

Slowly he straightened, his dark brows drawing together as he stared down at her. "Whoa, honey, let's backtrack a little. What do you mean, 'keep the ranch going'? The ranch is already dead."

"No, it isn't," she denied, stubbornness creeping into her tone. "I still have some cattle left."

"Where?" His disbelief was evident.

"In the south pasture. The fence on the east side needs repair, and I haven't—" She faltered at the growing anger in his dark face. Why should it matter to him? Their land joined mostly on the north; his cattle weren't in any danger of straying.

"Let's backtrack a little further," he said tightly. "Who's supposed to be working this herd?"

So that was it. He didn't believe her, because he knew there were no cowhands working here any longer. "I'm working the herd," she threw back at him, her face closed and proud. He couldn't have made it any plainer that he didn't consider her either capable or willing when it came to ranch work.

He looked her up and down, his brows lifting as he surveyed her. She knew exactly what he saw, because she'd deliberately created the image. He saw mauve-lacquered toenails, white high-heeled sandals, crisp white linen pants and the white silk shirt, damp now, from contact with his wet clothes. Suddenly Michelle realized that she was damp all along the front, and hectic color rose to burn along her cheekbones, but she lifted her chin just that much higher. Let him look, damn him.

"Nice," he drawled. "Let me see your hands."

Instinctively her hands curled into fists and she glared at him. "Why?"

He moved like a striking rattler, catching her wrist and holding her clenched hand in front of him. She pulled back, twisting in an effort to escape him, but he merely tightened his grip and pried her fingers open, then turned her palm to the light. His face was still and expressionless as he looked down at her hand for a long minute; then he caught her other hand and examined it, too. His grip gentled, and he traced his fingertips over the scratches and half-healed blisters, the forming calluses.

Michelle sat with her lips pressed together in a grim line, her face deliberately blank. She wasn't ashamed of her hands; work inevitably left its mark on human flesh, and she'd found something healing in the hard physical demands the ranch made on her. But no matter how honorable those marks, when John looked at them it was as if he'd stripped her naked and looked at her, as if he'd exposed something private. She didn't want him to know so much about her; she didn't want that intense interest turned on her. She didn't want pity from anyone, but she especially didn't want him to soften toward her.

Then his gaze lifted, those midnight eyes examining every inch of her proud, closed expression, and every instinct in her shrilled an alarm. Too late! Perhaps it had been too late from the moment he'd stepped onto the porch. From the beginning she'd sensed the tension in him, the barely controlled anticipation that she had mistaken for his usual hostility. Rafferty wasn't used to waiting for any woman he wanted, and she'd held him off for ten years. The only time she'd been truly safe from him had been during her brief marriage, when the distance between Philadelphia and central Florida had been more than hundreds of miles; it had been the distance between two totally different life-styles, in both form and substance. But now she was back within reach, and this time she was vulnerable. She was broke, she was alone, and she owed him a hundred thousand dollars. He probably expected it to be easy.

"You didn't have to do it alone," he finally said, his deep voice somehow deeper and quieter. He still held her hands, and his rough thumbs still moved gently, caressingly, over her palms, as he stood and drew her to her feet. She realized that at no time had he hurt her; he'd held her against her will, but he hadn't hurt her. His touch was gentle, but she knew without even trying that she wouldn't be able to pull away from him until he voluntarily let her go.

Her only defense was still the light mockery she'd used against him from the beginning. She gave him a bright, careless smile. "Of course I did. As you so charmingly pointed out, I'm not exactly being trampled by all my friends rushing to my rescue, am I?"

His upper lip curled with contempt for those "friends." He'd never had any patience with the bored and idle rich. "You could've come to me."

Again she gave him that smile, knowing he hated it. "But it would take so *long* to work off a hundred-thousand-dollar debt in that fashion, wouldn't it? You know how I hate being bored. A really good prostitute makes—what?—a hundred dollars a throw? Even if you were up to three times a day, it would still take about a year—"

Swift, dark fury burned in his eyes, and he finally released her hands, but only to move his grip to her shoulders. He held her still while he raked his gaze down her body again. "Three times a day?" he asked with that deceptive softness, looking at her breasts and hips. "Yeah, I'm up to it. But you forgot about interest, honey. I charge a lot of interest."

She quivered in his hands, wanting to close her eyes against that look. She'd taunted him rashly, and he'd turned her words back on her. Yes, he was capable of it. His sexual drive was so fierce that he practically burned with it, attracting women like helpless moths. Desperately she dredged up the control to keep smiling, and managed a little shrug despite his hands on her shoulders. "Thanks anyway, but I prefer shoveling manure."

If he'd lost control of his temper then she would have breathed easier, knowing that she still had the upper hand, by however slim a margin. If she could push him away with insults, she'd be safe. But though his hands tightened a little on her shoulders, he kept a tight rein on his temper.

"Don't push too hard, honey," he advised quietly. "It wouldn't take much for me to show you right now what you really like. You'd be better off telling me just how in hell you think you're going to keep this ranch alive by yourself."

For a moment her eyes were clear and bottomless, filled with a desperation he wasn't quite certain he'd seen. Her skin was tight over her chiseled cheekbones; then the familiar cool mockery and defiance were back, her eyes mossy and opaque, her lips curling a little in the way that made him want to shake her. "The ranch is my problem," she said, dismissing the offer of aid implicit in his words. She knew the price he'd demand for his help. "The only way it concerns you is in how you want the debt repaid."

Finally he released her shoulders and propped himself against the desk again, stretching his long legs and crossing his booted feet at the ankle. "A hundred thousand is a lot of money. It wasn't easy to come up with that much cash."

She didn't need to be told that. John might be a millionaire in assets, but a rancher's money is tied up in land and stock, with the profits constantly being plowed back into the ranch. Cash simply wasn't available for wasting on frivolities. Her jaw tightened. "When do you want your money?" she demanded. "Now or later?"

His dark brows lifted. "Considering the circumstances, you should be trying to sweeten me up instead of snapping at me. Why haven't you just put the ranch and cattle up for sale? You can't run the place anyway, and at least then you'd have money to live on until you find another meal ticket."

"I *can* run it," she flared, turning pale. She had to; it was all she had.

"No way, honey."

"Don't call me honey!" The ragged fury of her own voice startled her. He called every woman "honey." It was a careless endearment that meant nothing, because so many other women had heard it from him. She couldn't stand to think of him lying in the dark with another woman, his voice lazy and dark as they talked and he called her "honey."

He caught her chin in his big, rough hand, turning her face up to his while his thumb rubbed over her lower lip. "I'll call you whatever I want...*honey*, and you'll keep your mouth shut, because you owe me a lot of money that you can't repay. I'm going to think awhile about that debt and what we're going to do about it. Until I decide, why don't you think about this?"

Too late she tried to draw her head back, but he still held her chin, and his warm mouth settled over hers before she could jerk free. Her eyes closed as she tried to ignore the surge of pleasure in her midsection, tried to ignore the way his lips moved over hers and his tongue probed for entrance. If anything, this was worse than before, because now he was kissing her with a slow assurance that beguiled even as he demanded. She tried to turn her head away, but he forestalled the movement, spreading his legs and pulling her inside the cradle of his iron-muscled thighs. Michelle began shaking. Her hands flattened against his chest, but she could feel his heartbeat pulsing strongly against her palm, feel the accelerated rhythm of it, and she wanted to sink herself into him. Slowly he wedged her head back against his shoulder, his fingers woven into her hair as he held her. There was no way she could turn her head away from him now, and slowly she began to give way to his will. Her mouth opened beneath his, accepting the slow thrust of his tongue as he penetrated her in that small way and filled her with his taste.

He kissed her with shattering absorption, as if he couldn't get enough of her. Even the dim thought that he must have practised his technique with hundreds of women didn't lessen its power. She was utterly wrapped around by him, overwhelmed by his touch and scent and taste, her body tingling and aching with both pleasure and the need to have more of him. She wanted him; she'd always wanted him. He'd been an obsession with her from the moment she had seen him, and she'd spent most of the past ten years running from the power of that obsession, only to wind up practically at his mercy anyway—if he had any mercy.

He lifted his head in slow motion, his dark eyes heavy lidded, his mouth moist from kissing her. Blatant satisfaction was written across his hard face as he surveyed her. She was lying limply against him, her face dazed with pure want, her lips red and swollen. Very gently he put her away from him, holding her with his hands on her waist until she was steady on her feet; then he got to his own feet.

As always when he towered over her, Michelle automatically retreated a step. Frantically she searched for control, for something to say to him to deny the response she'd just given him, but what could she say that he'd believe? She couldn't have been more obvious! But then, neither could he. It was useless to try to regain lost ground, and she wasn't going to waste time trying. All she could do was try to put a halt to things now.

Her face was pale as she faced him, her hands twisted together in a tight knot. ''I won't sleep with

you to pay that debt, no matter what you decide. Did
you come here tonight expecting to whisk me straight
up to bed, assuming that I'd choose to turn whore for
you?''

He eyed her sharply. "The thought crossed my
mind. I was willing."

"Well, I'm not!" Breath rushed swiftly in and out
of her lungs as she tried to control the outrage that
burned in her at the insult. She had to control it; she
couldn't afford to fall apart now.

"I'm glad, because I've changed my mind," he said
lazily.

"Gosh, that's big of you!" she snapped.

"You'll go to bed with me, all right, but it won't be
because of any money you owe me. When the time
comes, you'll spread your legs for me because you
want me just the way I want you."

The way he was looking at her made her shiver, and
the image his rough words provoked shot through her
brain like lightning. He would use her up and toss her
away, just as he had all those other women, if she let
him get too close to her. "Thanks, but no thanks. I've
never gone in for group sex, and that's what it would
be like with you!"

She wanted to make him angry, but instead he
cupped her knotted-up hands in his palm and lightly
rubbed his thumb over her knuckles. "Don't worry, I
can guarantee there'll just be the two of us between the
sheets. Settle down and get used to the idea. I'll be
back out tomorrow to look over the ranch and see
what needs to be done—"

"No," she interrupted fiercely, jerking her hands
from his grip. "The ranch is mine. I can handle it on
my own."

"Honey, you've never even handled a checkbook on your own. Don't worry about it; I'll take care of everything."

His amused dismissal set her teeth on edge, more because of her own fear that he was right than anything else. "I don't want you to take care of everything!"

"You don't know what you want," he replied, leaning down to kiss her briefly on the mouth. "I'll see you tomorrow."

Just like that he turned and walked out of the room, and after a moment Michelle realized he was leaving. She ran after him and reached the front door in time to see him sprinting through the downpour to his truck.

He didn't take her seriously. Well, why should he? Michelle thought bitterly. No one else ever had, either. She leaned on the doorframe and watched him drive away; her shaky legs needed the extra support. Why now? For years she'd kept him at a distance with her carefully manufactured hostility, but all of a sudden her protective barrier had shattered. Like a predator, he'd sensed her vulnerability and moved in for the kill.

Quietly she closed the door, shutting out the sound of rain. The silent house enclosed her, an empty reminder of the shambles of her life.

Her jaw clenched as she ground her teeth together, but she didn't cry. Her eyes remained dry. She couldn't afford to waste her time or strength indulging in useless tears. Somehow she had to hold on to the ranch, repay that debt, and hold off John Rafferty. . . .

The last would be the hardest of all, because she'd be fighting against herself. She didn't want to hold him off; she wanted to creep into his iron-muscled arms and feel them close around her. She wanted to feed her hunger for him, touch him as she'd never allowed herself to do, immerse herself in the man. Guilt arose in her throat, almost choking her. She'd married another man wanting John, loving John, *obsessed* with John; somehow Roger, her ex-husband, had sensed it, and his jealousy had turned their marriage into a nightmare.

Her mind burned with the memories, and to distract herself she walked briskly into the kitchen and prepared dinner for one; in this case, a bowl of cornflakes in milk. It was also what she'd had for breakfast, but her nerves were too raw to permit any serious cooking. She was actually able to eat half of the bowlful of cereal before she suddenly dropped the spoon and buried her face in her hands.

All her life she'd been a princess, the darling, pampered apple of her parents' eyes, born to them when they were both nearing forty and had given up hope of ever having children. Her mother had been a gentle, vague person who had passed straight from her father's keeping into that of her husband, and thought that a woman's role in life was to provide a comfortable, loving home for her husband, who supported her. It wasn't an unusual outlook for her generation, and Michelle didn't fault her mother for it. Langley Cabot had protected and spoiled both his wife and his daughter; that was the way life was supposed to be, and it was a source of pride to him that he supported them very well indeed. When her mother died, Michelle had become the recipient of all that protective devotion. Langley had wanted her to have the best of everything; he had wanted her to be happy, and to his way of thinking he had failed as a father and provider if she weren't.

In those days Michelle had been content to let her father shower her with gifts and luxuries. Her life had been humming along just as she had always expected, until the day Langley had turned her world upside down by selling the Connecticut house where she'd grown up, and moved her down to a cattle ranch in central Florida, not far from the Gulf coast. For the first time in her life, Langley had been unmoved by her pleas. The cattle ranch was his dream come true, the answer to some deeply buried need in him that had been hidden under silk shirts, pin-striped suits and business appointments. Because he'd wanted it so badly, he had ignored Michelle's tears and tantrums and jovially assured her that before long she'd have new friends and would love the ranch as much as he did.

In that, he was partially right. She made new friends, gradually became accustomed to the heat, and even enjoyed life on a working cattle ranch. Langley had completely remodeled the old ranch house when he'd bought it, to ensure that his beloved daughter wasn't deprived in any way of the comfort she was accustomed to. So she'd adjusted, and even gone out of her way to assure him of her contentment. He deserved his dream, and she had felt ashamed that she'd tried to talk him out of it. He did so much to make her happy, the least she could do was return as much of the effort as she could.

Then she'd met John Rafferty. She couldn't believe that she'd spent ten years running from him, but it was true. She'd hated him and feared him and loved him all at once, with a teenager's wildly passionate obses-

sion, but she had always seen one thing very clearly:
he was more than she could handle. She had never
daydreamed of being the one woman who could tame
the rake; she was far too vulnerable to him, and he was
too strong. He might take her and use her, but she
wasn't woman enough to hold him. She was spoiled
and pampered; he didn't even like her. In self-defense,
she had devoted herself to making him dislike her even
more to make certain he never made a move on her.

She had gone to an exclusive women's college back
east, and after graduation had spent a couple of weeks
with a friend who lived in Philadelphia. During that
visit she'd met Roger Beckman, scion of one of the
oldest and richest families in town. He was tall and
black haired, and he even had a trim mustache. His
resemblance to John was slight, except for those
points, and Michelle couldn't say that she had con-
sciously married Roger because he reminded her of
John, but she was very much afraid that subconsciously she had done exactly that.

Roger was a lot of fun. He had a lazy manner about
him, his eyes wrinkled at the edges from smiling so
much, and he loved organized crazy games, like scav-
enger hunts. In his company Michelle could forget
about John and simply have fun. She was genuinely
fond of Roger, and came to love him as much as she
would ever love any man who wasn't John Rafferty.
The best thing she could do was forget about John,
put him behind her, and get on with her life. After all,
there had never been anything between them except
her own fantasies, and Roger absolutely adored her.
So she had married him, to the delight of both her father and his parents.

It was a mistake that had almost cost her her life.

At first everything had been fine. Then Roger had begun to show signs of jealousy whenever Michelle was friendly to another man. Had he sensed that she didn't love him as she should? That he owned only the most superficial part of her heart? Guilt ate at her even now, because Roger's jealousy hadn't been groundless. He hadn't been able to find the true target, so he'd lashed out whenever she smiled at any man, danced with any man.

The scenes had gotten worse, and one night he'd actually slapped her during a screaming fight after a party; she'd made the mistake of speaking to the same man twice while they raided the buffet table. Shocked, her face burning, Michelle had stared at her husband's twisted features and realized that his jealousy had driven him out of control. For the first time, she was afraid of him.

His action had shocked Roger, too, and he'd buried his face in her lap, clinging to her as he wept and begged her forgiveness. He'd sworn never to hurt her again; he'd said he would rather cut off his own hands than hurt her. Shaken to the core, Michelle did what thousands of women did when their husbands turned on them: she forgave him.

But it wasn't the last time. Instead, it got worse.

Michelle had been too ashamed and shocked to tell anyone, but finally she couldn't take any more and pressed charges against him. To her horror, his parents quietly bought off everyone involved, and Michelle was left without a legal leg to stand on, all evidence destroyed. Come hell or high water, the Beckmans would protect their son.

Finally she tried to leave him, but she had gotten no further than Baltimore before he caught up with her, his face livid with rage. It was then that Michelle realized he wasn't quite sane; his jealousy had pushed him over the edge. Holding her arm in a grip that left bruises for two weeks, he made the threat that kept her with him for the next two years: if she left him again, he'd have her father killed.

She hadn't doubted him, nor did she doubt that he'd get away with it; he was too well protected by his family's money and prestige, by a network of old family friends in the law business. So she'd stayed, terrified that he might kill her in one of his rages, but not daring to leave. No matter what, she had to protect her father.

But finally she found a way to escape. Roger had beaten her with a belt one night. But his parents had been in Europe on vacation, and by the time they found out about the incident it was too late to use their influence. Michelle had crept out of the house, gone to a hospital where her bruises and lacerations were treated and recorded, and she'd gotten copies of the records. Those records had bought her a divorce.

The princess would carry the scars to her grave.

Chapter 3

The telephone rang as Michelle was nursing her second cup of coffee, watching the sun come up and preparing herself for another day of chores that seemed to take more and more out of her. Dark circles lay under her heavy-lidded eyes, testimony to hours of twisting restlessly in bed while her mind insisted on replaying every word John had said, every sensation his mouth and hands had evoked. His reputation was well earned, she had thought bitterly in the early hours. Lady-killer. His touch was burningly tender, but he was hell on his women anyway.

She didn't want to answer the phone, but she knew John well enough to know he never gave up once he set his mind on something. He'd be back, and she knew it. If that was him on the telephone, he'd come over if she didn't answer. She didn't feel up to dealing with him in person, so she picked up the receiver and muttered a hello.

"Michelle, darling."

She went white, her fingers tightening on the receiver. Had she conjured him up by thinking about him the night before? She tried *not* to think of him, to keep him locked in the past, but sometimes the nightmare memories surfaced, and she felt again the terror of being so alone and helpless, with no one she could trust to come to her aid, not even her father.

"Roger," she said faintly. There was no doubt. No one but her ex-husband said her name in that caressing tone, as if he adored her.

His voice was low, thick. "I need you, darling. Come back to me, please. I'm begging. I promise I'll never hurt you again. I'll treat you like a princess—"

"No," she gasped, groping for a chair to support her shaking legs. Cold horror made her feel sick. How could he even suggest that she come back?

"Don't say that, please," he groaned. "Michelle, Mother and Dad are dead. I need you now more than ever. I thought you'd come for their funeral last week, but you stayed away, and I can't stand it any longer. If you'll just come back I swear everything will be different—"

"We're divorced," she broke in, her voice thin with strain. Cold sweat trickled down her spine.

"We can be remarried. Please, darling—"

"No!" The thought of being remarried to him filled her with so much revulsion that she couldn't even be polite. Fiercely she struggled for control. "I'm sorry about your parents; I didn't know. What happened?"

"Plane crash." Pain still lingered in his hoarse voice. "They were flying up to the lake and got caught in a storm."

"I'm sorry," she said again, but even if she'd known in time to attend the funeral, she never would have gone. She would never willingly be in Roger's presence again.

He was silent a moment, and she could almost see him rub the back of his neck in the unconscious nervous gesture she'd seen so many times. "Michelle, I still love you. Nothing's any good for me without you. I swear, it won't be the same as it was; I'll never hurt you again. I was just so damned jealous, and I know now I didn't have any reason."

But he did! she thought, squeezing her eyes shut as guilt seeped in to mix with the raw terror evoked by simply hearing his voice. Not physically, but had there been any day during the past ten years when she hadn't thought of John Rafferty? When part of her hadn't been locked away from Roger and every other man because they weren't the heartbreaker who'd stolen her heart?

"Roger, don't," she whispered. "It's over. I'll never come back. All I want to do now is work this ranch and make a living for myself."

He made a disgusted sound. "You shouldn't be working that dinky little ranch! You're used to much better than that. I can give you anything you want."

"No," she said softly. "You can't. I'm going to hang up now. Goodbye, and please don't call me again." Very gently she replaced the receiver, then stood by the phone with her face buried in her hands. She couldn't stop trembling, her mind and body reeling with the ramifications of what he'd told her. His parents were dead, and she had been counting on them to control him. That was the deal she'd made with them; if they would keep Roger away from her, she wouldn't release the photos and medical report to the press, who would have a field day with the scandal. Imagine, a Beckman of Philadelphia nothing but a common wife-beater! That evidence had kept her father safe from Roger's insane threats, too, and now he was forever beyond Roger's reach. She had lived in hell to protect her father, knowing that Roger was capable of doing exactly what he'd threatened, and knowing after the first incident that his parents would make certain Roger was protected, no matter what.

She had honestly liked her in-laws until then, but her affection had died an irrevocable death when they had bought Roger out of trouble the first time he'd really hurt her. She had known their weakness then, and she had forced herself to wait. There was no one to help her; she had only herself. Once she had been desperate enough to mention it to her father, but he'd become so upset that she hadn't pushed it, and in only a moment he'd convinced himself that she'd been exaggerating. Marriage was always an adjustment, and Michelle was spoiled, highly strung. Probably it was just an argument over some minor thing, and the young couple would work things out.

The cold feeling of aloneness had spread through her, but she hadn't stopped loving him. He loved her, she knew he did, but he saw her as more of a doll than a human being. His perfect, loving darling. He couldn't accept such ugliness in her life. She had to be happy, or it would mean he'd failed her in some basic way as a father, protector and provider. For his own sake, he had to believe she was happy. That was his weakness, so she had to be strong for both of them. She had to protect him, and she had to protect herself.

There was no way she would ever go back to Roger. She had dealt with the nightmares and put them behind her; she had picked up the pieces of her life and gone on, not letting the memories turn her into a frightened shell. But the memories, and the fear, were still there, and all it took was hearing Roger's voice to make her break out in a cold sweat. The old feeling of vulnerability and isolation swept over her, making her feel sick.

She jerked around, wrenching herself from the spell, and dashed what was left of her coffee down the drain. The best thing was to be active, to busy herself with whatever came to hand. That was the way she'd handled it when she had finally managed to get away from Roger, globe-trotting for two years because her father had thought that would take her mind off the divorce, and she had let the constant travel distract her. Now she had real work to do, work that left her exhausted and aching but was somehow healing, because it was the first worthwhile work she'd ever done.

It had been eating at him all morning.

He'd been in a bad mood from the moment he'd gotten out of bed, his body aching with frustration, as if he were some randy teenager with raging hormones. He was a long way from being a teenager, but his hormones were giving him hell, and he knew exactly why. He hadn't been able to sleep for remembering the way she'd felt against him, the sweetness of her taste and the silky softness of her body. And she wanted him, too; he was too experienced to be mistaken about something like that. But he'd pushed too hard, driven by ten years of having an itch he couldn't scratch, and she'd balked. He'd put her in the position of paying him with her body, and she hadn't liked that. What woman would? Even the ones who were willing usually wanted a pretty face put on it, and Michelle was haughtier than most.

But she hadn't looked haughty the day before. His frown grew darker. She had tried, but the old snooty coldness was missing. She was dead broke and had nowhere to turn. Perhaps she was scared, wondering what she was going to do without the cushion of money that had always protected her. She was practically helpless, having no job skills or talents other than social graces, which weren't worth a hell of a lot on the market. She was all alone on that ranch, without the people to work it.

He made a rough sound and pulled his horse's head around. "I'll be back later," he told Nev, nudging the horse's flanks with his boot heels.

Nev watched him ride away. "Good riddance," he muttered. Whatever was chewing on the boss had put him in the worst mood Nev had ever seen; it would be a relief to work without him.

John's horse covered the distance with long, easy strides; it was big and strong, seventeen hands high, and inclined to be a bit stubborn, but they had fought that battle a long time ago. Now the animal accepted the mastery of the iron-muscled legs and strong, steady hands of his rider. The big horse liked a good run, and he settled into a fast, smooth rhythm as they cut across pastures, his pounding hooves sending clods of dirt flying.

The more John thought about it, the less he liked it. She'd been trying to work that ranch by herself. It didn't fit in with what he knew of Michelle, but her fragile hands bore the marks. He had nothing but contempt for someone who disdained good honest work and expected someone else to do it for them, but something deep and primitive inside him was infuriated at the idea of Michelle even trying to manage the backbreaking chores around the ranch. Damn it, why hadn't she asked for help? Work was one thing, but no one expected her to turn into a cowhand. She wasn't strong enough; he'd held her in his arms, felt the delicacy of her bones, the greyhound slenderness of her build. She didn't need to be working cattle any more than an expensive thoroughbred should be used to plow a field. She could get hurt, and it might be days before anyone found her. He'd always been disgusted with Langley for spoiling and protecting her, and with Michelle for just sitting back and accepting it as her due, but suddenly he knew just how Langley had felt. He gave a disgusted snort at himself, making the horse flick his ears back curiously at the sound, but the hard fact was that he didn't like the idea of Michelle's trying to work that ranch. It was a man's work, and more than one man, at that.

Well, he'd take care of all that for her, whether she liked it or not. He had the feeling she wouldn't, but she'd come around. She was too used to being taken care of, and, as he'd told her, now it was his turn.

Yesterday had changed everything. He'd felt her response to him, felt the way her mouth had softened and shaped itself to his. She wanted him, too, and the knowledge only increased his determination to have her. She had tried to keep him from seeing it; that acid tongue of hers would have made him lose his temper if he hadn't seen the flicker of uncertainty in her eyes. It was so unusual that he'd almost wanted to bring back the haughtiness that aggravated him so much....

Almost, but not quite. She was vulnerable now, vulnerable to him. She might not like it, but she needed him. It was an advantage he intended to use.

There was no answer at the door when he got to the ranch house, and the old truck was missing from its customary parking place in the barn. John put his fists on his hips and looked around, frowning. She had probably driven into town, though it was hard to think that Michelle Cabot was willing to let herself be seen in that kind of vehicle. It was her only means of transportation, though, so she didn't have much choice.

Maybe it was better that she was gone; he could check around the ranch without her spitting and hissing at him like an enraged cat, and he'd look at those cattle in the south pasture. He wanted to know just how many head she was running, and how they looked. She couldn't possibly handle a big herd by herself, but for her sake he hoped they were in good shape, so she could get a fair price for them. He'd handle it himself, make certain she didn't get rooked. The cattle business wasn't a good one for beginners.

He swung into the saddle again. First he checked the east pasture, where she had said the fence was down. Whole sections of it would have to be replaced, and he made mental notes of how much fencing it would take. The entire ranch was run-down, but fencing was critical; it came first. Lush green grass covered the east pasture; the cattle should be in it right now. The south pasture was probably overgrazed, and the cattle would show it, unless the herd was small enough that the south pasture could provide for its needs.

It was a couple of hours before he made it to the south pasture. He reined in the horse as he topped a small rise that gave him a good view. The frown snapped into place again, and he thumbed his hat onto the back of his head. The cattle he could see scattered over the big pasture didn't constitute a big herd, but made for far more than the small one he'd envisioned. The pasture was badly overgrazed, but scattered clumps of hay testified to Michelle's efforts to feed her herd. Slow-rising anger began to churn in him as he thought of her wrestling with heavy bales of hay; some of them probably weighed more than she did.

Then he saw her, and in a flash the anger rose to boiling point. The old truck was parked in a clump of trees, which was why he hadn't noticed it right off, and she was down there struggling to repair a section of fencing by herself. Putting up fencing was a two-man job; one person couldn't hold the barbed wire securely enough, and there was always the danger of the wire backlashing. The little fool! If the wire got wrapped around her, she wouldn't be able to get out of it without help, and those barbs could really rip a person up. The thought of her lying tangled and bleeding in a coil of barbed wire made him both sick and furious.

He kept the horse at an easy walk down the long slope to where she was working, deliberately giving himself time to get control of his temper. She looked up and saw him, and even from the distance that still separated them he could see her stiffen. Then she turned back to the task of hammering a staple into the fence post, her jerky movements betraying her displeasure at his presence.

He dismounted with a fluid, easy motion, never taking his gaze from her as he tied the reins to a low-hanging tree branch. Without a word he pulled the strand of wire to the next post and held it taut while Michelle, equally silent, pounded in another staple to hold it. Like him, she had on short leather work gloves, but her gloves were an old pair of men's gloves that had been left behind and were far too big for her, making it difficult for her to pick up the staples, so she had pulled off the left glove. She could handle the staples then, but the wire had already nicked her unprotected flesh several times. He saw the angry red scratches; some of which were deep enough for blood to well, and he wanted to shake her until her teeth rattled.

"Don't you have any better sense than to try to put up fencing on your own?" he rasped, pulling another strand tight.

She hammered in the staple, her expression closed. "It has to be done. I'm doing it."

"Not anymore, you aren't."

His flat statement made her straighten, her hand closing tightly around the hammer. "You want the payment right away," she said tonelessly, her eyes sliding to the cattle. She was a little pale, and tension pulled the skin tight across her high cheekbones.

"If that's what I have to do." He pried the hammer from her grip, then bent to pick up the sack of staples. He walked over to the truck, then reached in the open window and dropped them onto the floorboard. Then he lifted the roll of barbed wire onto the truck bed. "That'll hold until I can get my men out here to do it right. Let's go."

It was a good thing he'd taken the hammer away from her. Her hands balled into fists. "I don't want your men out here doing it right! This is still my land,

and I'm not willing to pay the price you want for your help.''

''I'm not giving you a choice.'' He took her arm, and no matter how she tried she couldn't jerk free of those long, strong fingers as he dragged her over to the truck, opened the door and lifted her onto the seat. He released her then, slamming the door and stepping back.

''Drive carefully, honey. I'll be right behind you.''

She had to drive carefully; the pasture was too rough for breakneck speed, even if the old relic had been capable of it. She knew he was easily able to keep up with her on his horse, though she didn't check the rearview mirror even once. She didn't want to see him, didn't want to think about selling the cattle to pay her debt. That would be the end of the ranch, because she'd been relying on that money to keep the ranch going.

She'd hoped he wouldn't come back today, though it had been a fragile hope at best. After talking to Roger that morning, all she wanted was to be left alone. She needed time by herself to regain her control, to push all the ugly memories away again, but John hadn't given her that time. He wanted her, and like any predator he'd sensed her vulnerability and was going to take advantage of it.

She wanted to just keep driving, to turn the old truck down the driveway, hit the road and keep on going. She didn't want to stop and deal with John, not now. The urge to run was so strong that she almost did it, but a glance at the fuel gauge made her mouth twist wryly. If she ran, she'd have to do it on foot, either that or steal John's horse.

She parked the truck in the barn, and as she slid off the high seat John walked the horse inside, ducking his head a little to miss the top of the doorframe. "I'm going to cool the horse and give him some water," he said briefly. "Go on in the house. I'll be there in a minute."

Was postponing the bad news for a few minutes supposed to make her feel better? Instead of going straight to the house, she walked down to the end of the driveway and collected the mail. Once the mailbox had been stuffed almost every day with magazines, catalogs, newspapers, letters from friends, business papers, but now all that came was junk mail and bills. It was odd how the mail reflected a person's solvency, as if no one in the world wanted to communicate with someone who was broke. Except for past-due bills, of course. Then the communications became serious. A familiar envelope took her attention, and a feeling of dread welled in her as she trudged up to the house. The electric bill was past due; she'd already had one late notice, and here was another one. She had to come up with the money fast, or the power would be disconnected. Even knowing what it was, she opened the envelope anyway and scanned the notice. She had ten days to bring her account up to date. She checked the date of the notice; it had taken three days to reach her. She had seven days left.

But why worry about the electricity if she wouldn't have a ranch? Tiredness swept over her as she entered the cool, dim house and simply stood for a moment, luxuriating in the relief of being out of the broiling sun. She shoved the bills and junk mail into the same drawer of the entry table where she had put the original bill and the first late notice; she never forgot about them, but at least she could put them out of sight.

She was in the kitchen, having a drink of water, when she heard the screen door slam, then the sharp sound of boot heels on the oak parquet flooring as he came down the hallway. She kept drinking, though she was acutely aware of his progress through the house. He paused to look into the den, then the study. The slow, deliberate sound of those boots as he came closer made her shiver in reaction. She could see him in her mind's eye; he had a walk that any drugstore cowboy would kill for: that loose, long-legged, slim-hipped saunter, tight buttocks moving up and down. It was a walk that came naturally to hell-raisers and heart-breakers, and Rafferty was both.

She knew the exact moment when he entered the kitchen, though her back was to him. Her skin suddenly tingled, as if the air had become charged, and the house no longer seemed so cool.

"Let me see your hand." He was so close behind her that she couldn't turn without pressing against him, so she remained where she was. He took her left hand in his and lifted it.

"They're just scratches," she muttered.

She was right, but admitting it didn't diminish his anger. She shouldn't have any scratches at all; she shouldn't be trying to repair fencing. Her hand lay in his bigger, harder one like a pale, fragile bird, too tired to take flight, and suddenly he knew that the image was exactly right. She was tired.

He reached around her to turn on the water, then thoroughly soaped and rinsed her hand. Michelle hurriedly set the water glass aside, before it slipped from her trembling fingers, then stood motionless, with her head bowed. He was very warm against her back; she felt completely surrounded by him, with his arms around her while he washed her hand with the gentleness a mother would use to wash an infant. That gentleness staggered her senses, and she kept her head bent precisely to prevent herself from letting it drop back against his shoulder to let him support her.

The soap was rinsed off her hand now, but still he held it under the running water, his fingers lightly stroking. She quivered, trying to deny the sensuality of his touch. He was just washing her hand! The water was warm, but his hand was warmer, the rough calluses rasping against her flesh as he stroked her with a lover's touch. His thumb traced circles on her sensitive palm, and Michelle felt her entire body tighten. Her pulse leaped, flooding her with warmth. "Don't," she said thickly, trying unsuccessfully to pull free.

He turned off the water with his right hand, then moved it to her stomach and spread his fingers wide, pressing her back against his body. His hand was wet; she felt the dampness seeping through her shirt in front, and the searing heat of him at her back. The smell of horse and man rose from that seductive heat. Everything about the man was a come-on, luring women to him.

"Turn around and kiss me," he said, his voice low, daring her to do it.

She shook her head and remained silent, her head bent.

He didn't push it, though they both knew that if he had, she wouldn't have been able to resist him. Instead he dried her hand, then led her to the downstairs bathroom and made her sit on the lid of the toilet while he thoroughly cleaned the scratches with antiseptic. Michelle didn't flinch from the stinging; what did a few scratches matter, when she was going to lose the ranch? She had no other home, no other place she wanted to be. After being virtually imprisoned in that plush penthouse in Philadelphia, she needed the feeling of space around her. The thought of living in a city again made her feel stifled and panicky, and she would have to live in some city somewhere to get a job, since she didn't even have a car to commute. The old truck in the barn wouldn't hold up to a long drive on a daily basis.

John watched her face closely; she was distracted about something, or she would never have let him tend her hand the way he had. After all, it was something she could easily have done herself, and he'd done it merely to have an excuse to touch her. He wanted to know what she was thinking, why she insisted on working this ranch when it had to be obvious even to her that it was more than she could handle. It simply wasn't in character for her.

"When do you want the money?" she asked dully.

His mouth tightened as he straightened and pulled her to her feet. "Money isn't what I want," he replied.

Her eyes flashed with green fire as she looked at him. "I'm not turning myself into a whore, even for you! Did you think I'd jump at the chance to sleep with you? Your reputation must be going to your head...*stud*."

He knew people called him that, but when Michelle said it, the word dripped with disdain. He'd always hated that particular tone, so icy and superior, and it made him see red now. He bent down until his face was level with hers, their noses almost touching, and his black eyes were so fiery that she could see gold sparks in them. "When we're in bed, honey, you can decide for yourself about my reputation."

"I'm not going to bed with you," she said through clenched teeth, spacing the words out like dropping stones into water.

"The hell you're not. But it won't be for this damned ranch." Straightening to his full height again, he caught her arm. "Let's get that business settled right now, so it'll be out of the way and you can't keep throwing it in my face."

"You're the one who put it on that basis," she shot back as they returned to the kitchen. He dropped several ice cubes in a glass and filled it with water, then draped his big frame on one of the chairs. She watched his muscular throat working as he drained the glass, and a weak, shivery feeling swept over her. Swiftly she looked away, cursing her own powerful physical response to the mere sight of him.

"I made a mistake," he said tersely, putting the glass down with a thump. "Money has nothing to do with it. We've been circling each other from the day we met, sniffing and fighting like cats in heat. It's time we did something about it. As for the debt, I've decided what I want. Deed that land you were going to sell over to me instead, and we'll be even."

It was just like him to divide her attention like that, so she didn't know how to react or what to say. Part of her wanted to scream at him for being so smugly certain she would sleep with him, and part of her was flooded with relief that the debt had been settled so easily. He could have ruined her by insisting on cash, but he hadn't. He wasn't getting a bad deal, by any means; it was good, rich pastureland he was obtaining, and he knew it.

It was a reprieve, one she hadn't expected, and she didn't know how to deal with it, so she simply sat and stared at him. He waited, but when she didn't say anything he leaned back in his chair, his hard face becoming even more determined. "There's a catch," he drawled.

The high feeling of relief plummeted, leaving her sick and empty. "Let me guess," she said bitterly, shoving her chair back and standing. So it had all come down to the same thing after all.

His mouth twisted wryly in self-derision. "You're way off, honey. The catch is that you let me help you. My men will do the hard labor from now on, and if I even hear of you trying to put up fencing again, you'll be sitting on a pillow for a month."

"If your men do my work, I'll still be in debt to you."

"I don't consider it a debt; I call it helping a neighbor."

"I call it a move to keep me obligated!"

"Call it what you like, but that's the deal. You're one woman, not ten men; you're not strong enough to take care of the livestock and keep the ranch up, and you don't have the money to afford help. You're mighty short on options, so stop kicking. It's your fault, anyway. If you hadn't liked to ski so much, you wouldn't be in this position."

She drew back, her green eyes locked on him. Her face was pale. "What do you mean?"

John got to his feet, watching her with the old look that said he didn't much like her. "I mean that part of the reason your daddy borrowed the money from me was so he could afford to send you to St. Moritz with your friends last year. He was trying to hold his head above water, but that didn't matter to you as much as living in style, did it?''

She had been pale before, but now she was deathly white. She stared at him as if he'd slapped her, and too late he saw the shattered look in her eyes. Swiftly he rounded the table, reaching for her, but she shrank away from him, folding in on herself like a wounded animal. How ironic that she should now be struggling to repay a debt made to finance a trip she hadn't wanted! All she'd wanted had been time alone in a quiet place, a chance to lick her wounds and finish recovering from a brutal marriage, but her father had thought resuming a life of trips and shopping with her friends would be better, and she'd gone along with him because it had made him happy.

"I didn't even want to go," she said numbly, and to her horror tears began welling in her eyes. She didn't want to cry; she hadn't cried in years, except once when her father died, and she especially didn't want to cry in front of Rafferty. But she was tired and off balance, disturbed by the phone call from Roger that morning, and this just seemed like the last straw. The hot tears slipped silently down her cheeks.

"God, don't," he muttered, wrapping his arms around her and holding her to him, her face pressed against his chest. It was like a knife in him to see those tears on her face, because in all the time he'd known her, he'd never before seen her cry. Michelle Cabot had faced life with either a laugh or a sharp retort, but never with tears. He found he preferred an acid tongue to this soundless weeping.

For just a moment she leaned against him, letting him support her with his hard strength. It was too tempting; when his arms were around her, she wanted to forget everything and shut the world out, as long as he was holding her. That kind of need frightened her, and she stiffened in his arms, then pulled free. She swiped her palms over her cheeks, wiping away the dampness, and stubbornly blinked back the remaining tears.

His voice was quiet. "I thought you knew."

She threw him an incredulous look before turning away. What an opinion he had of her! She didn't mind his thinking she was spoiled; her father had spoiled her, but mostly because he'd enjoyed doing it so much. Evidently John not only considered her a common whore, but a stupid one to boot.

"Well, I didn't. And whether I knew or not doesn't change anything. I still owe you the money."

"We'll see my lawyer tomorrow and have the deed drawn up, and that'll take care of the damned debt. I'll be here at nine sharp, so be ready. A crew of men will be here in the morning to take care of the fencing and get the hay out to the herd."

He wasn't going to give in on that, and he was right; it *was* too much for her, at least right now. She couldn't do it all simply because it was too much for one person to do. After she fattened up the beef cattle and sold them off, she'd have some capital to work with and might be able to hire someone part-time.

"All right. But keep a record of how much I owe you. When I get this place back on its feet, I'll repay every penny." Her chin was high as she turned to face him, her green eyes remote and proud. This didn't solve all her problems, but at least the cattle would be cared for. She still had to get the money to pay the bills, but that problem was hers alone.

"Whatever you say, honey," he drawled, putting his hands on her waist.

She only had time for an indrawn breath before his mouth was on hers, as warm and hard as she remembered, his taste as heady as she remembered. His hands tightened on her waist and drew her to him; then his arms were around her, and the kiss deepened, his tongue sliding into her mouth. Hunger flared, fanned into instant life at his touch. She had always known that once she touched him, she wouldn't be able to get enough of him.

She softened, her body molding itself to him as she instinctively tried to get close enough to him to feed that burning hunger. She was weak where he was concerned, just as all women were. Her arms were clinging around his neck, and in the end it was he who broke the kiss and gently set her away from him.

"I have work to get back to," he growled, but his eyes were hot and held dark promises. "Be ready tomorrow."

"Yes," she whispered.

Chapter 4

Two pickup trucks came up the drive not long after sunrise, loaded with fencing supplies and five of John's men. Michelle offered them all a cup of fresh coffee, which they politely refused, just as they refused her offer to show them around the ranch. John had probably given them orders that she wasn't to do anything, and they were taking it seriously. People didn't disobey Rafferty's orders if they wanted to continue working for him, so she didn't insist, but for the first time in weeks she found herself with nothing to do.

She tried to think what she'd done with herself before, but years of her life were a blank. What *had* she done? How could she fill the hours now, if working on her own ranch was denied her?

John drove up shortly before nine, but she had been ready for more than an hour and stepped out on the porch to meet him. He stopped on the steps, his dark eyes running over her in heated approval. "Nice," he murmured just loud enough for her to hear. She looked the way she should always look, cool and elegant in a pale yellow silk surplice dress, fastened only by two white buttons at the waist. The shoulders were lightly padded, emphasizing the slimness of her body, and a white enamel peacock was pinned to her lapel. Her sunshine hair was sleeked back into a demure twist; oversized sunglasses shielded her eyes. He caught the tantalizing fragrance of some softly bewitching perfume, and his body began to heat. She was aristocratic and expensive from her head to her daintily shod feet; even her underwear would be silk, and he wanted to strip every stitch of it away from her, then stretch her out naked on his bed. Yes, this was exactly the way she should look.

Michelle tucked her white clutch under her arm and walked with him to the car, immensely grateful for the sunglasses covering her eyes. John was a hard-working rancher, but when the occasion demanded he could dress as well as any Philadelphia lawyer. Any clothing looked good on his broad-shouldered, slim-hipped frame, but the severe gray suit he wore seemed to heighten his masculinity instead of restraining it. All hint of waviness had been brushed from his black hair. Instead of his usual pickup truck he was driving a dark gray two-seater Mercedes, a sleek beauty that made her think of the Porsche she had sold to raise money after her father had died.

"You said your men were going to help me," she said expressionlessly as he turned the car onto the highway several minutes later. "You didn't say they were going to take over."

He'd put on sunglasses, too, because the morning sun was glaring, and the dark lenses hid the probing look he directed at her stiff profile. "They're going to do the heavy work."

"After the fencing is repaired and the cattle are moved to the east pasture, I can handle things from there."

"What about dipping, castrating, branding, all the things that should've been done in the spring? You can't handle that. You don't have any horses, any men, and you sure as hell can't rope and throw a young bull from that old truck you've got."

Her slender hands clenched in her lap. Why did he have to be so right? She couldn't do any of those things, but neither could she be content as a useless ornament. "I know I can't do those things by myself, but I can help."

"I'll think about it," he answered noncommittally, but he knew there was no way in hell he'd let her. What could she do? It was hard, dirty, smelly, bloody work. The only thing she was physically strong enough to do was brand calves, and he didn't think she could stomach the smell or the frantic struggles of the terrified little animals.

"It's my ranch," she reminded him, ice in her tone. "Either I help, or the deal's off."

John didn't say anything. There was no point in arguing. He simply wasn't going to let her do it, and that was that. He'd handle her when the time came, but he didn't expect much of a fight. When she saw what was involved, she wouldn't want any part of it. Besides, she couldn't possibly like the hard work she'd been doing; he figured she was just too proud to back down now.

It was a long drive to Tampa, and half an hour passed without a word between them. Finally she said, "You used to make fun of my expensive little cars."

He knew she was referring to the sleek Mercedes, and he grunted. Personally, he preferred his pickup. When it came down to it, he was a cattle rancher and not much else, but he was damned good at what he did, and his tastes weren't expensive. "Funny thing about bankers," he said by way of explanation. "If they think you don't need the money all that badly, they're eager to loan it to you. Image counts. This thing is part of the image."

"And the members of your rotating harem prefer it, too, I bet," she gibed. "Going out on the town lacks something when you do it in a pickup."

"I don't know about that. Ever done it in a pickup?" he asked softly, and even through the dark glasses she could feel the impact of his glance.

"I'm sure *you* have."

"Not since I was fifteen." He chuckled, ignoring the biting coldness of her comment. "But a pickup never was your style, was it?"

"No," she murmured, leaning her head back. Some of her dates had driven fancy sports cars, some had driven souped-up Fords and Chevys, but it hadn't made any difference what they'd driven, because she hadn't made out with any of them. They had been nice boys, most of them, but none of them had been John Rafferty, so it hadn't mattered. He was the only man she'd ever wanted. Perhaps if she'd been older when she'd met him, or if she'd been secure enough in her own sexuality, things might have been different. What would have happened if she hadn't initiated those long years of hostility in an effort to protect herself from an attraction too strong for her to handle? What if she'd tried to get him interested in her, instead of warding him off?

Nothing, she thought tiredly. John wouldn't have wasted his time with a naive eighteen-year-old. Maybe later, when she'd graduated from college, the situation might have changed, but instead of coming home after graduation she had gone to Philadelphia ... and met Roger.

They were out of the lawyer's office by noon; it hadn't been a long meeting. The land would be surveyed, the deed drawn up, and John's ranch would increase by quite a bit, while hers would shrink, but she was grateful that he'd come up with that solution. At least now she still had a chance.

His hand curled warmly around her elbow as they walked out to the car. "Let's have lunch. I'm too hungry to wait until we get home."

She was hungry, too, and the searing heat made her feel lethargic. She murmured in agreement as she fumbled for her sunglasses, missing the satisfied smile that briefly curled his mouth. John opened the car door and held it as she got in, his eyes lingering on the length of silken leg exposed by the movement. She promptly restored her skirt to its proper position and crossed her legs as she settled in the seat, giving him a questioning glance when he continued to stand in the open door. "Is something wrong?"

"No." He closed the door and walked around the car. Not unless she counted the way looking at her made him so hot that a deep ache settled in his loins. She couldn't move without making him think of making love to her. When she crossed her legs, he thought of uncrossing them. When she pulled her skirt down, he thought of pulling it up. When she leaned back the movement thrust her breasts against her lapels, and he wanted to tear the dress open. Damn, what a dress! It wrapped her modestly, but the silk kissed every soft curve just the way he wanted to do, and all morning long it had been teasing at him that the damned thing was fastened with only those two buttons. Two buttons! He had to have her, he thought savagely. He couldn't wait much longer. He'd already waited ten years, and his patience had ended. It was time.

The restaurant he took her to was a posh favorite of the city's business community, but he didn't worry about needing a reservation. The maître d' knew him, as did most of the people in the room, by sight and reputation if not personally. They were led across the crowded room to a select table by the window.

Michelle had noted the way so many people had watched them. "Well, this is one," she said dryly.

He looked up from the menu. "One what?"

"I've been seen in public with you once. Gossip has it that any woman seen with you twice is automatically assumed to be sleeping with you."

His mustache twitched as he frowned in annoyance. "Gossip has a way of being exaggerated."

"Usually, yes."

"And in this case?"

"You tell me."

He put the menu aside, his eyes never leaving her. "No matter what gossip says, you won't have to worry about being just another member of a harem. While we're together, you'll be the only woman in my bed."

Her hands shook, and Michelle quickly put her menu on the table to hide that betraying quiver.

"You're assuming a lot," she said lightly in an effort to counteract the heat she could feel radiating from him.

"I'm not assuming anything. I'm planning on it." His voice was flat, filled with masculine certainty. He had reason to be certain; how many women had ever refused him? He projected a sense of overwhelming virility that was at least as seductive as the most expert technique, and from what she'd heard, he had that, too. Just looking at him made a woman wonder, made her begin dreaming about what it would be like to be in bed with him.

"Michelle, darling!"

Michelle couldn't stop herself from flinching at that particular phrase, even though it was spoken in a lilting female voice rather than a man's deeper tones. Quickly she looked around, grateful for the interruption despite the endearment she hated; when she recognized the speaker, gratefulness turned to mere politeness, but her face was so schooled that the approaching woman didn't catch the faint nuances of expression.

"Hello, Bitsy, how are you?" she asked politely as John got to his feet. "This is John Rafferty, my neighbor. John, this is Bitsy Sumner, from Palm Beach. We went to college together."

Bitsy's eyes gleamed as she looked at John, and she held her hand out to him. "I'm so glad to meet you, Mr. Rafferty."

Michelle knew Bitsy wouldn't pick it up, but she saw the dark amusement in John's eyes as he gently took the woman's faultlessly manicured and bejeweled hand in his. Naturally he'd seen the way Bitsy was looking at *him*. It was a look he'd probably been getting since puberty.

"Mrs. Sumner," he murmured, noting the diamond-studded wedding band on her left hand. "Would you like to join us?"

"Only for a moment," Bitsy sighed, slipping into the chair he held out. "My husband and I are here with some business associates and their wives. He says it's good business to socialize with them occasionally, so we flew in this morning. Michelle, dear, I haven't seen you in so long! What are you doing on this side of the state?"

"I live north of here," Michelle replied.

"You must come visit. Someone mentioned just the other day that it had been forever since we'd seen you! We had the most fantastic party at Howard Cassa's villa last month; you should have come."

"I have too much work to do, but thank you for the invitation." She managed to smile at Bitsy, but she understood that Bitsy hadn't been inviting her to visit them personally; it was just something that people said, and probably her old acquaintances were curious about why she had left their circle.

Bitsy shrugged elegantly. "Oh, work, schmurk. Let someone else take care of it for a month or so. You need to have some fun! Come to town, and bring Mr. Rafferty with you." Bitsy's gaze slid back to John, and that unconsciously hungry look crawled into her eyes again. "You'd enjoy it, Mr. Rafferty, I promise. Everyone needs a break from work occasionally, don't you think?"

His brows lifted. "Occasionally."

"What sort of business are you in?"

"Cattle. My ranch adjoins Michelle's."

"Oh, a *rancher*!"

Michelle could tell by Bitsy's fatuous smile that the other woman was lost in the romantic images of cowboys and horses that so many people associated with ranching, ignoring or simply not imagining the backbreaking hard work that went in to building a successful ranch. Or maybe it was the rancher instead of the ranch that made Bitsy look so enraptured. She was looking at John as if she could eat him alive. Michelle put her hands in her lap to hide them because she had to clench her fists in order to resist slapping Bitsy so hard she'd never even think of looking at John Rafferty again.

Fortunately good manners drove Bitsy back to her own table after a few moments. John watched her sway through the tangle of tables, then looked at Michelle with amusement in his eyes. "Who in hell would call a grown woman *Bitsy*?"

It was hard not to share his amusement. "I think her real name is Elizabeth, so Bitsy is fairly reasonable as a nickname. Of course, she was the ultimate preppy in college, so it fits."

"I thought it might be an indication of her brain power," he said caustically; then the waiter approached to take their orders, and John turned his attention to the menu.

Michelle could only be grateful that Bitsy hadn't been able to remain with them. The woman was one of the worst gossips she'd ever met, and she didn't feel up to hearing the latest dirt on every acquaintance they had in common. Bitsy's particular circle of friends were rootless and a little savage in their pursuit of entertainment, and Michelle had always made an effort to keep her distance from them. It hadn't always been possible, but at least she had never been drawn into the center of the crowd.

After lunch John asked if she would mind waiting while he contacted one of his business associates. She started to protest, then remembered that his men were taking care of the cattle today; she had no reason to hurry back, and, in truth, she could use the day off. The physical strain had been telling on her. Besides, this was the most time she'd ever spent in his company, and she was loathe to see the day end. They weren't arguing, and if she ignored his arrogant certainty that they were going to sleep together, the day had really been rather calm. "I don't have to be back at any certain time," she said, willing to let him decide when they would return.

As it happened, it was after dark before they left Tampa. John's meeting had taken up more time than he'd expected, but Michelle hadn't been bored, because he hadn't left her sitting in the reception area. He'd taken her into the meeting with him, and it had been so interesting that she hadn't been aware of the hours slipping past. It was almost six when they finished, and by then John was hungry again; it was another two hours before they were actually on their way.

Michelle sat beside him, relaxed and a little drowsy. John had stayed with coffee, because he was driving, but she'd had two glasses of wine with her meal, and her bones felt mellow. The car was dark, illuminated only by the dash lights, which gave a satanic cast to his hard-planed face, and the traffic on U.S. 19 was light. She snuggled down into the seat, making a comment only when John said something that required an answer.

Soon they ran into a steady rain, and the rhythmic motion of the windshield wipers added to her drowsiness. The windows began to fog, so John turned the air conditioning higher. Michelle sat up, hugging her arms as the cooler air banished her drowsiness. Her silk dress didn't offer much warmth. He glanced at her, then pulled to the side of the road.

"Why are we stopping?"

"Because you're cold." He shrugged out of his suit jacket and draped it around her, enveloping her in the transferred heat and the smell of his body. "We're almost two hours from home, so why don't you take a nap? That wine's getting to you, isn't it?"

"Mmmm." The sound of agreement was distinctly drowsy. John touched her cheek gently, watching as her eyelids closed, as if her lashes were too heavy for her to hold them open a moment longer. Let her sleep, he thought. She'd be recovered from the wine by the time they got home. His loins tightened. He wanted her awake and responsive when he took her to bed. There was no way he was going to sleep alone tonight. All day long he'd been fighting the need to touch her, to feel her lying against him. For ten years she'd been in his mind, and he wanted her. As difficult and spoiled as she was, he wanted her. Now he understood what made men want to pamper her, probably from the day she'd been placed in her cradle. He'd just taken his place in line, and for his reward he'd have her in his bed, her slim, silky body open for his pleasure. He knew she wanted him; she was resisting him for some reason he couldn't decipher, perhaps only a woman's instinctive hesitance.

Michelle usually didn't sleep well. Her slumber was frequently disturbed by dreams, and she hadn't been able to nap with even her father anywhere nearby. Her subconscious refused to relax if any man was in the vicinity. Roger had once attacked her in the middle of the night, when she'd been soundly asleep, and the trauma of being jerked from a deep, peaceful sleep into a nightmare of violence had in some ways been worse than the pain. Now, just before she slept, she realized with faint surprise that the old uneasiness wasn't there tonight. Perhaps the time had come to heal that particular hurt, too, or perhaps it was that she felt so unutterably safe with John. His coat warmed her; his nearness surrounded her. He had touched her in passion and in anger, but his touch had never brought pain. He tempered his great strength to handle a woman's softness, and she slept, secure in the instinctive knowledge that she was safe.

His deep, dark-velvet voice woke her. "We're home, honey. Put your arms around my neck."

She opened her eyes to see him leaning in the open door of the car, and she gave him a sleepy smile. "I slept all the way, didn't I?"

"Like a baby." He brushed her mouth with his, a brief, warm caress; then his arms slid behind her neck and under her thighs. She gasped as he lifted her, grabbing him around the neck as he'd instructed. It was still raining, but his coat kept most of the dampness from her as he closed the car door and carried her swiftly through the darkness.

"I'm awake now; I could've walked," she protested, her heart beginning a slow, heavy thumping as she responded to his nearness. He carried her so easily, leaping up the steps to the porch as if she weighed no more than a child.

"I know," he murmured, lifting her a little so he could bury his face in the curve of her neck. Gently he nuzzled her jaw, drinking in the sweet, warm fragrance of her skin. "Mmmm, you smell good. Are you clear from the wine yet?"

The caress was so tender that it completely failed to alarm her. Rather, she felt coddled, and the feeling of utter safety persisted. He shifted her in his arms to open the door, then turned sideways to carry her through. Had he thought she was drunk? "I was just sleepy, not tipsy," she clarified.

"Good," he whispered, pushing the door closed and blocking out the sound of the light rain, enveloping them in the dark silence of the house. She couldn't see anything, but he was warm and solid against her, and it didn't matter that she couldn't see. Then his mouth was on hers, greedy and demanding, convincing her lips to open and accept the shape of his, accept the inward thrust of his tongue. He kissed her with burning male hunger, as if he wanted to draw all the sweetness and breath out of her to make it his own, as if the need was riding him so hard that he couldn't get close enough. She couldn't help responding to that need, clinging to him and kissing him back with a sudden wildness, because the very rawness of his male hunger called out to everything in her that was female and ignited her own fires.

He hit the light switch with his elbow, throwing on the foyer light and illuminating the stairs to the right. He lifted his mouth briefly, and she stared up at him in the dim light, her senses jolting at the hard, grim expression on his face, the way his skin had tightened across his cheekbones. "I'm staying here tonight," he muttered harshly, starting up the stairs with her still in his arms. "This has been put off long enough."

He wasn't going to stop; she could see it in his face. She didn't want him to stop. Every pore in her body cried out for him, drowning out the small voice of caution that warned against getting involved with a heartbreaker like John Rafferty. Maybe it had been a useless struggle anyway; it had always been between them, this burning hunger that now flared out of control.

His mouth caught hers again as he carried her up the stairs, his muscle-corded arms holding her weight easily. Michelle yielded to the kiss, sinking against him. Her blood was singing through her veins, heating her, making her breasts harden with the need for his touch. An empty ache made her whimper, because it was an ache that only he could fill.

He'd been in the house a lot over the years, so the location of her room was no mystery to him. He carried her inside and laid her on the bed, following her down to press her into the mattress with his full weight. Michelle almost cried out from the intense pleasure of feeling him cover her with his body. His arm stretched over her head, and he snapped on one of the bedside lamps; he looked at her, and his black eyes filled with masculine satisfaction as he saw the glaze of passion in her slumberous eyes, the trembling of her pouty, kiss-stung lips.

Slowly, deliberately, he levered his knee between hers and spread her legs, then settled his hips into the cradle formed by her thighs. She inhaled sharply as she felt his hardness through the layers of their clothing. Their eyes met, and she knew he'd known before the day even began that he would end it in her bed. He was tired of waiting, and he was going to have her. He'd been patient all day, gentling her by letting her get accustomed to his presence, but now his patience was at an end, and he knew she had no resistance left to offer him. All she had was need.

"You're mine." He stated his possession baldly, his voice rough and low. He raised his weight on one elbow, and with his free hand unbuttoned the two buttons at her waist, spreading the dress open with the deliberate air of a man unwrapping a gift he'd wanted for a long time. The silk caught at her hips, pinned by his own weight. He lifted his hips and pushed the edges of the dress open, baring her legs, then re-settled himself against her.

He felt as if his entire body would explode as he looked at her. She had worn neither bra nor slip; the silk dress was lined, hiding from him all day the fact that the only things she had on beneath that wisp of fabric were her panty hose and a minute scrap of lace masquerading as panties. If he'd known that her breasts were bare under her dress, there was no way he could have kept himself from pulling those lapels apart and touching, tasting, nor could he stop himself now. Her breasts were high and round, the skin satiny, her coral-colored nipples small and already tightly beaded. With a rough sound he bent his head and sucked strongly at her, drawing her nipple into his mouth and molding his lips to that creamy, satiny flesh. He cupped her other breast in his hand, gently kneading it and rubbing the nipple with his thumb. A high, gasping cry tore from her throat, and she arched against his mouth, her hands digging into his dark hair to press his head into her. Her breasts were so firm they were almost hard, and the firmness excited him even more. He had to taste the other one, surround himself with the sweet headiness of her scent and skin.

Slowly Michelle twisted beneath him, plucking now at the back of his shirt in an effort to get rid of the fabric between them. She needed to feel the heat and power of his bare skin under her hands, against her body, but his mouth on her breasts was driving her mad with pleasure, and she couldn't control herself enough to strip the shirt away. Every stroke of his tongue sent wildfire running along her nerves, from her nipples to her loins, and she was helpless to do anything but feel.

Then he left her, rising up on his knees to tear at his shirt and throw it aside. His shoes, socks, pants and underwear followed, flung blindly away from the bed, and he knelt naked between her spread thighs. He stripped her panty hose and panties away, leaving her open and vulnerable to his penetration.

For the first time, she felt fear. It had been so long for her, and sex hadn't been good in her marriage anyway. John leaned over her, spreading her legs further, and she felt the first shock of his naked flesh as he positioned himself for entry. He was so big, his muscled body dominating her smaller, softer one completely. She knew from harsh experience how helpless a woman was against a man's much greater strength; John was stronger than most, bigger than most, and he was intent on the sexual act as males have been from the beginning of time. He was quintessentially male, the sum and substance of masculine aggression and sexuality. Panic welled in her, and her slim, delicate hand pressed against him, her fingers sliding into the curling dark hair that covered his chest. The black edges of fear were coming closer.

Her voice was thready, begging for reassurance. "John? Don't hurt me, please."

He froze, braced over her on the threshold of entry. Her warm, sweet body beckoned him, moistly ready for him, but her eyes were pleading. Did she expect pain? Good God, who could have hurt her? The seeds of fury formed deep in his mind, shunted aside for now by the screaming urges of his body. For now, he had to have her. "No, baby," he said gently, his dark voice so warm with tenderness that the fear in her eyes faded. "I won't hurt you."

He slid one arm under her, leaning on that elbow and raising her so her nipples were buried in the hair on his chest. Again he heard that small intake of breath from her, an unconscious sound of pleasure. Their eyes locked, hers misty and soft, his like black fire, as he tightened his buttocks and very slowly, very carefully, began to enter her.

Michelle shuddered as great ripples of pleasure washed through her, and her legs climbed his to wrap around his hips. A soft, wild cry tore from her throat, and she shoved her hand against her mouth to stifle the sound. Still his black eyes burned down at her. "No," he whispered. "Take your hand away. I want to hear you, baby. Let me hear how good it feels to you."

Still there was that slow, burning push deep into her, her flesh quivering as she tried to accommodate him. Panic seized her again. "Stop! John, please, no more! You're...I can't..."

"Shh, shh," he soothed, kissing her mouth, her eyes, nibbling at the velvety lobes of her ears. "It's okay, baby, don't worry. I won't hurt you." He continued soothing her with kisses and soft murmurs, and though every instinct in him screamed to bury himself in her to the hilt, he clamped down on those urges with iron control. There was no way he was going to hurt her, not with the fear he'd seen in the misty green depths of her eyes. She was so delicate and silky, and so tight around him that he could feel the gentle pulsations of adjustment. His eyes closed as pure pleasure shuddered through him.

She was aroused, but not enough. He set about exciting her with all the sensual skill he possessed, holding her mouth with deep kisses while his hands gently stroked her, and he began moving slowly inside her. So slow, holding himself back, keeping his strokes shallow even though every movement wrung new degrees of ecstasy from him. He wanted her mindless with need.

Michelle felt her control slipping away by degrees, and she didn't care. Control didn't matter, nothing mattered but the heat that was consuming her body and mind, building until all sense of self was gone and she was nothing but a female body, twisting and surging beneath the overpowering male. A powerful tension had her in its grip, tightening, combining with the heat as it swept her inexorably along. She was burning alive, writhing helplessly, wild little pleading sobs welling up and escaping. John took them into his own mouth, then put his hand between their bodies, stroking her. She trembled for a moment on the crest of a great wave; then she was submerged in exploding sensation. He held her safely, her heaving body locked in his arms while he thrust deeply, giving her all the pleasure he could.

When it was over she was limp and sobbing, drenched with both her sweat and his. "I didn't know," she said brokenly, and tears tracked down her face. He murmured to her, holding her tightly for a moment, but he was deep inside her now, and he couldn't hold back any longer. Sliding his hands beneath her hips, he lifted her up to receive his deep, powerful thrusts.

Now it was she who held him, cradling him in her body and with her arms tight around him; he cried out, a deep, hoarse sound, blind and insensible to everything but the great, flooding force of his pleasure.

It was quiet for a long time afterward. John lay on top of her, so sated and relaxed that he couldn't tolerate the idea of moving, of separating his flesh from hers. It wasn't until she stirred, gasping a little for breath, that he raised himself on his elbows and looked down at her.

Intense satisfaction, mingled with both gentleness and a certain male arrogance, was written on his face as he leaned above her. He smoothed her tangled hair back from her face, stroking her cheeks with his fingers. She looked pale and exhausted, but it was the sensuous exhaustion of a woman who has been thoroughly satisfied by her lover. He traced the shape of her elegant cheekbones with his lips, his tongue dipping out to sneak tastes that sent little ripples of arousal through him again.

Then he lifted his head again, curiosity burning in his eyes. "You've never enjoyed it before, have you?"

A quick flush burned her cheeks, and she turned her head on the pillow, staring fixedly at the lamp. "I suppose that does wonders for your ego."

She was withdrawing from him, and that was the last thing he wanted. He decided to drop the subject for the time being, but there were still a lot of questions that he intended to have answered. Right now she was in his arms, warm and weak from his lovemaking, just the way he was going to keep her until she became used to his possession and accepted it as fact.

She was his now.

He'd take care of her, even spoil her. Why not? She was made to be pampered and indulged, at least up to a point. She'd been putting up a good fight to work this ranch, and he liked her guts, but she wasn't cut out for that type of life. Once she realized that she didn't have to fight anymore, that he was going to take care of her, she'd settle down and accept it as the natural order of things.

He didn't have money to waste on fancy trips, or to drape her in jewels, but he could keep her in comfort and security. Not only that, he could guarantee that the sheets on their bed would stay hot. Even now, so soon after having her, he felt the hunger and need returning.

Without a word he began again, drawing her down with him into a dark whirlpool of desire and satisfaction. Michelle's eyes drifted shut, her body arching in his arms. She had known instinctively, years ago, that it would be like this, that even her identity would be swamped with the force of his passion. In his arms she lost herself and became only his woman.

Chapter 5

Michelle woke early, just as the first gray light of dawn was creeping into the room. The little sleep she'd gotten had been deep and dreamless for a change, but she was used to sleeping alone; the unaccustomed presence of a man in her bed had finally nudged her awake. A stricken look edged into her eyes as she looked over at him, sprawled on his stomach with one arm curled under the pillow and the other arm draped across her naked body.

How easy she'd been for him. The knowledge ate at her as she gingerly slipped from the bed, taking care not to wake him. He might sleep for hours yet; he certainly hadn't had much sleep during the night.

Her legs trembled as she stood, the soreness in her thighs and deep in her body providing yet another reminder of the past night, as if she needed any further confirmation of her memory. Four times. He'd taken her four times, and each time it had seemed as if the

pleasure intensified. Even now she couldn't believe
how her body had responded to him, soaring wildly
out of her control. But he'd controlled himself, and
her, holding her to the rhythm he set in order to pro-
long their lovemaking. Now she knew that all the talk
about him hadn't been exaggerated; both his virility
and his skill had been, if anything, underrated.

Somehow she had to come to terms with the un-
pleasant fact that she had allowed herself to become
the latest of his one-night stands. The hardest fact to
face wasn't that she'd been so easily seduced, but her
own piercing regret that such ecstasy wouldn't last.
Oh, he might come back...but he wouldn't stay. In
time he'd become bored with her and turn his preda-
tory gaze on some other woman just as he always had
before.

And she'd go on loving him, just as she had before.

Quietly she got clean underwear from the dresser
and her bathrobe from the adjoining bath, but she
went to the bathroom down the hall to take a shower.
She didn't want the sound of running water to awaken
him. Right now she needed time to herself, time to
gather her composure before she faced him again. She
didn't know what to say, how to act.

The stinging hot water eased some of the soreness
from her muscles, though a remaining ache reminded
her of John's strength with every step she took. After
showering she went down to the kitchen and started
brewing a fresh pot of coffee. She was leaning against
the cabinets, watching the dark brew drip into the pot,
when the sound of motors caught her attention.
Turning to look out the window, she saw the two
pickup trucks from John's ranch pull into the yard.
The same men who had been there the day before got

out; one noticed John's car parked in front of the house and poked his buddy in the ribs, pointing. Even from that distance Michelle could hear the muffled male laughter, and she didn't need any help imagining their comments. The boss had scored again. It would be all over the county within twenty-four hours. In the manner of men everywhere, they were both proud and slightly envious of their boss's sexual escapades, and they'd tell the tale over and over again.

Numbly she turned back to watch the coffee dripping; when it finished, she filled a big mug, then wrapped her cold fingers around the mug to warm them. It had to be nerves making her hands so cold. Quietly she went upstairs to look into her bedroom, wondering if he would still be sleeping.

He wasn't, though evidently he'd awoken only seconds before. He propped himself up on one elbow and ran his hand through his tousled black hair, narrowing his eyes as he returned her steady gaze. Her heart lurched painfully. He looked like a ruffian, with his hair tousled, his jaw darkened by the overnight growth of beard, his bare torso brown and roped with the steely muscles that were never found on a businessman. She didn't know what she'd hoped to see in his expression: desire, possibly, even affection. But whatever she'd wanted to see wasn't there. Instead his face was as hard as always, measuring her with that narrowed gaze that made her feel like squirming. She could feel him waiting for her to move, to say something.

Her legs were jerky, but she managed not to spill the coffee as she walked into the room. Her voice was only slightly strained. "Congratulations. All the gossip doesn't give you due credit. My, my, you're really something when you decide to score; I didn't even think of saying no. Now you can go home and put another notch in your bedpost."

His eyes narrowed even more. He sat up, ignoring the way the sheet fell below his waist, and held out his hand for the coffee mug. When she gave it to him, he turned it and drank from the place where she'd been sipping, then returned it to her, his eyes never leaving hers.

"Sit down."

She flinched a little at his hard, raspy, early-morning voice. He saw the small movement and reached out to take her wrist, making coffee lap alarmingly close to the rim of the mug. Gently but inexorably he drew her down to sit facing him on the edge of the bed.

He kept his hand on her wrist, his callused thumb rubbing over the fine bones and delicate tracery of veins. "Just for the record, I don't notch bedposts. Is that what's got your back up this morning?"

She gave a small defensive shrug, not meeting his eyes.

She'd withdrawn from him again; his face was grim as he watched her, trying to read her expression. He remembered the fear in her last night, and he wondered who'd put it there. White-hot embers of rage began to flicker to life at the thought of some bastard abusing her in bed, hurting her. Women were vulnerable when they made love, and Michelle especially wouldn't have the strength to protect herself. He had to get her to talk, or she'd close up on him completely. "It had been a long time for you, hadn't it?"

Again she gave that little shrug, as if hiding behind the movement. Again he probed, watching her face.

"You didn't enjoy sex before." He made it a statement, not a question.

Finally her eyes darted to his, wary and resentful. "What do you want, a recommendation? You know that was the first time I'd . . . enjoyed it."

"Why didn't you like it before?"

"Maybe I just needed to go to bed with a stud," she said flippantly.

"Hell, don't give me that," he snapped, disgusted. "Who hurt you? Who made you afraid of sex?"

"I'm not afraid," she denied, disturbed by the idea that she might have let Roger warp her to such an extent. "It was just . . . well, it had been so long, and you're a big man. . . ." Her voice trailed off, and abruptly she flushed, her gaze sliding away from him.

He watched her thoughtfully; considering what he'd learned about her last night and this morning, it was nothing short of a miracle that she hadn't knocked his proposal and half his teeth down his throat when he'd suggested she become his mistress as payment of the debt. It also made him wonder if her part in the breakup of Mike Webster's marriage hadn't been blown out of all proportion; after all, a woman who didn't enjoy making love wasn't likely to be fast and easy.

It was pure possessiveness, but he was glad no other man had pleased her the way he had; it gave him a hold on her, a means of keeping her by his side. He would use any weapon he had, because during the night he had realized that there was no way he could let her go. She could be haughty, bad-tempered and stubborn; she could too easily be spoiled and accept it as her due, though he'd be damned if he hadn't almost decided it *was* her due. She was proud and difficult, trying to build a stone wall around herself to keep him at a distance, like a princess holding herself aloof from the peasants, but he couldn't get enough of her. When they were making love, it wasn't the princess and the peasant any longer; they were a man and his woman, writhing and straining together, moaning with ecstasy. He'd never been so hungry for a woman before, so hot that he'd felt nothing and no one could have kept him away from her.

She seemed to think last night had been a casual thing on his part, that sunrise had somehow ended it. She was in for a surprise. Now that she'd given herself to him, he wasn't going to let her go. He'd learned how to fight for and keep what was his, but his single-minded striving over the years to build the ranch into one of the biggest cattle ranches in Florida was nothing compared to the intense possessiveness he felt for Michelle.

Finally he released her wrist, and she stood immediately, moving away from him. She sipped at the coffee she still held, and her eyes went to the window. "Your men got a big kick out of seeing your car still here this morning. I didn't realize they'd be back, since they put up the fencing yesterday."

Indifferent to his nakedness, he threw the sheet back and got out of bed. "They didn't finish. They'll do the rest of the job today, then move the herd to the east pasture tomorrow." He waited, then said evenly, "It bothers you that they know?"

"Being snickered about over a beer bothers me. It polishes up your image a little more, but all I'll be is the most recent in a long line of one-nighters for you."

"Well, everyone will know differently when you move in with me, won't they?" he asked arrogantly, walking into the bathroom. "How long will it take you to pack?"

Stunned, Michelle whirled to stare at him, but he'd already disappeared into the bathroom. The sound of the shower came on. Move in with him? If there was any limit to his gall, she hadn't seen it yet! She sat down on the edge of the bed, watching the bathroom door and waiting for him to emerge as she fought the uneasy feeling of sliding further and further down a precipitous slope. Control of her own life was slipping from her hands, and she didn't know if she could stop it. It wasn't just that John was so domineering, though he was; the problem was that, despite how much she wished it were different, she was weak where he was concerned. She wanted to be able to simply walk into his arms and let them lock around her, to rest against him and let him handle everything. She was so tired, physically and mentally. But if she let him take over completely, what would happen when he became bored with her? She would be right back where she'd started, but with a broken heart added to her problems.

The shower stopped running. An image of him formed in her mind, powerfully muscled, naked, dripping wet. Drying himself with her towels. Filling her bathroom with his male scent and presence. He wouldn't look diminished or foolish in her very feminine rose-and-white bathroom, nor would it bother him that he'd bathed with perfumed soap. He was so intensely masculine that female surroundings merely accentuated that masculinity.

She began to tremble, thinking of the things he'd done during the night, the way he'd made her feel. She hadn't known her body could take over like that, that she could revel in being possessed, and despite the outdated notion that a man could physically "possess" a woman, that was what had happened. She felt it, instinctively and deeply, the sensation sinking into her bones.

He sauntered from the bathroom wearing only a towel hitched low on his hips, the thick velvety fabric contrasting whitely with the bronzed darkness of his abdomen. His hair and mustache still gleamed wetly; a few drops of moisture glistened on his wide shoulders and in the curls that darkened his broad chest. Her mouth went dry. His body hair followed the tree of life pattern, with the tufts under his arms and curls across his chest, then the narrowing line that ran down his abdomen before spreading again at his groin. He was as superbly built as a triathlete, and she actually ached to touch him, to run her palms all over him.

He gave her a hard, level look. "Stop stalling and get packed."

"I'm not going." She tried to sound strong about it; if her voice lacked the volume she'd wanted, at least it was even.

"You'll be embarrassed if you don't have anything on besides that robe when I carry you into my house," he warned quietly.

"John—" She stopped, then made a frustrated motion with her hand. "I don't want to get involved with you."

"It's a little late to worry about that now," he pointed out.

"I know," she whispered. "Last night shouldn't have happened."

"Damn it to hell, woman, it should've happened a long time ago." Irritated, he dropped the towel to the floor and picked up his briefs. "Moving in with me is the only sensible thing to do. I normally work twelve hours a day, sometimes more. Sometimes I'm up all night. Then there's the paperwork to do in the evenings; hell, you know what it takes to run a ranch. When would I get over to see you? Once a week? I'll be damned if I'll settle for an occasional quickie."

"What about *my* ranch? Who'll take care of it while I make myself convenient to you whenever you get the urge?"

He gave a short bark of laughter. "Baby, if you lay down every time I got the urge, you'd spend the next year on your back. I get hard every time I look at you."

Involuntarily her eyes dropped down his body, and a wave of heat washed over her when she saw the proof of his words swelling against the white fabric of his underwear. She jerked her gaze away, swallowing to relieve the dry tightness of her throat. "I have to take care of my ranch," she repeated stubbornly, as if they were magic words that would keep him at bay.

He pulled on his pants, impatience deepening the lines that bracketed his mouth. "I'll take care of both ranches. Face facts, Michelle. You need help. You can't do it on your own."

"Maybe not, but I need to try. Don't you understand?" Desperation edged into her tone. "I've never had a job, never done anything to support myself, but I'm trying to learn. You're stepping right into Dad's shoes and taking over, handling everything yourself, but what happens to me when you get bored and move on to the next woman? I still won't know how to support myself!"

John paused in the act of zipping his pants, glaring at her. Damn it, what did she think he'd do, toss her out the door with a casual, "It's been fun, but I'm tired of you now?" He'd make certain she was on her feet, that the ranch was functioning on a profitable basis, if the day ever came when he looked at her and *didn't* want her. He couldn't imagine it. The desire for her consumed him like white-burning fire, sometimes banked, but never extinguished, heating his body and mind. He'd wanted her when she was eighteen and too young to handle him, and he wanted her now.

He controlled his anger and merely said, "I'll take care of you."

She gave him a tight little smile. "Sure." In her experience, people looked after themselves. Roger's parents had protected him to keep his slipping sanity from casting scandal on *their* family name. Her own father, as loving as he'd been, had ignored her plea for help because he didn't like to think his daughter was unhappy; it was more comfortable for him to decide she'd been exaggerating. The complaint she'd filed had disappeared because some judge had thought it would be advantageous to make friends with the powerful Beckmans. Roger's housekeeper had looked the other way because she liked her cushy well-paid job. Michelle didn't blame them, but she'd learned not to expect help, or to trust her life to others.

John snatched his shirt from the floor, his face dark with fury. "Do you want a written agreement?"

Tiredly she rubbed her forehead. He wasn't used to anyone refusing to obey him whenever he barked out an order. If she said yes, she would be confirming what he'd thought of her in the beginning, that her body could be bought. Maybe he even wanted her to say yes; then she'd be firmly under his control, bought and paid for. But all she said was, "No, that isn't what I want."

"Then what, damn it?"

Just his love. To spend the rest of her life with him. That was all.

She might as well wish for the moon.

"I want to do it on my own."

The harshness faded from his face. "You can't." Knowledge gave the words a finality that lashed at her.

"I can try."

The hell of it was, he had to respect the need to try, even though nature and logic said she wouldn't succeed. She wasn't physically strong enough to do what had to be done, and she didn't have the financial resources; she'd started out in a hole so deep that she'd been doomed to fail from the beginning. She would wear herself to the bone, maybe even get hurt, but in the end it would come full circle and she would need someone to take care of her. All he could do was wait, try to watch out for her, and be there to step in when everything caved in around her. By then she'd be glad to lean on a strong shoulder, to take the place in life she'd been born to occupy.

But he wasn't going to step back and let her pretend nothing had happened between them the night before. She was his now, and she had to understand that before he left. The knowledge had to be burned into her flesh the way it was burned into his, and maybe it would take a lesson in broad daylight for her to believe it. He dropped his shirt and slowly unzipped his pants, watching her. When he left, he'd leave his touch on her body and his taste in her mouth, and she'd feel him, taste him, think of him every time she climbed into this bed without him.

Her green eyes widened, and color bloomed on her cheekbones. Nervously she glanced at the bed, then back at him.

His heart began slamming heavily against his rib cage. He wanted to feel the firmness of her breasts in his hands again, feel her nipples harden in his mouth. She whispered his name as he dropped his pants and came toward her, putting his hands on her waist, which was so slender that he felt he might break her in two if he wasn't careful.

As he bent toward her, Michelle's head fell back as if it were too heavy for her neck to support. He instantly took advantage of her vulnerable throat, his mouth burning a path down its length. She had wanted to deny the force of what had happened, but her body was responding feverishly to him, straining against him in search of the mindless ecstasy he'd given her before. She no longer had the protection of ignorance. He was addictive, and she'd already become hooked. As he took her down to the bed, covering her with his heated nakedness, she didn't even think of denying him, or herself.

Are you on the pill?
No.
Damn. Then, *How long until your next period?*
Soon. Don't worry. The timing isn't right.
Famous last words. You'd better get a prescription.
I can't take the pill. I've tried; it makes me throw up all day long. Just like being pregnant.
Then we'll do something else. Do you want to take care of it, or do you want me to?

The remembered conversation kept replaying in her mind; he couldn't have made it plainer that he considered the relationship to be an ongoing one. He had been so matter-of-fact that it hadn't registered on her until later, but now she realized her acquiescent "I will" had acknowledged and accepted his right to make love to her. It hadn't hit her until he'd kissed her and had driven away that his eyes had been gleaming with satisfaction that had nothing to do with being physically sated.

She had some paperwork to do and forced herself to concentrate on it, but that only brought more problems to mind. The stack of unpaid bills was growing, and she didn't know how much longer she could hold her creditors off. They needed their money, too. She needed to fatten the cattle before selling them, but she didn't have the money for grain. Over and over she tried to estimate how much feed would cost, balanced against how much extra she could expect from the sale of heavier cattle. An experienced rancher would have known, but all she had to go on were the records her father had kept, and she didn't know how accurate they were. Her father had been wildly enthusiastic about his ranch, but he'd relied on his foreman's advice to run it.

She could ask John, but he'd use it as another chance to tell her that she couldn't do it on her own.

The telephone rang, and she answered it absently.

"Michelle, darling."

The hot rush of nausea hit her stomach, and she jabbed the button, disconnecting the call. Her hands were shaking as she replaced the receiver. Why wouldn't he leave her alone? It had been two years! Surely he'd had time to get over his sick obsession;

surely his parents had gotten him some sort of treatment!

The telephone rang again, the shrill tone filling her ears over and over. She counted the rings in a kind of frozen agony, wondering when he'd give up, or if her nerves would give out first. What if he just let it keep ringing? She'd have to leave the house or go screaming mad. On the eighteenth ring, she answered.

"Darling, don't hang up on me again, please," Roger whispered. "I love you so much. I have to talk to you or go crazy."

They were the words of a lover, but she was shaking with cold. Roger was already crazy. How many times had he whispered love words to her only moments after a burst of rage, when she was stiff with terror, her body already aching from a blow? But then he'd be sorry that he'd hurt her, and he'd tell her over and over how much he loved her and couldn't live without her.

Her lips were so stiff that she could barely form the words. "Please leave me alone. I don't want to talk to you."

"You don't mean that. You know I love you. No one has ever loved you as much as I do."

"I'm sorry," she managed.

"Why are you sorry?"

"I'm not going to talk to you, Roger. I'm going to hang up."

"Why can't you talk? Is someone there with you?"

Her hand froze, unable to remove the receiver from her ear and drop it onto its cradle. Like a rabbit numbed by a snake's hypnotic stare, she waited without breathing for what she knew was coming.

"Michelle! Is someone there with you?"

"No," she whispered. "I'm alone."

"You're lying! That's why you won't talk to me. Your lover is there with you, listening to every word you're saying."

Helplessly she listened to the rage building in his voice, knowing nothing she said would stop it, but unable to keep herself from trying. "I promise you, I'm alone."

To her surprise he fell silent, though she could hear his quickened breath over the wire as clearly as if he were standing next to her. "All right, I'll believe you. If you'll come back to me, I'll believe you."

"I can't—"

"There's someone else, isn't there? I always knew there was. I couldn't catch you, but I always knew!"

"No. There's no one. I'm here all alone, working in Dad's study." She spoke quickly, closing her eyes at the lie. It was the literal truth, that she was alone, but it was still a lie. There had always been someone else deep in her heart, buried at the back of her mind.

Suddenly his voice was shaking. "I couldn't stand it if you loved someone else, darling. I just couldn't. Swear to me that you're alone."

"I swear it." Desperation cut at her. "I'm completely alone, I swear!"

"I love you," Roger whispered, and hung up.

Wildly she ran for the bathroom, where she retched until she was empty and her stomach muscles ached from heaving. She couldn't take this again; she would have the phone number changed, keep it unlisted. Leaning against the basin, she wiped her face with a wet cloth and stared at her bloodless reflection in the mirror. She didn't have the money to pay for having her number changed and taken off the listing.

A shaky bubble of laughter escaped her trembling lips. The way things were going, the phone service would be disconnected soon because she couldn't pay her bill. That would certainly take care of the problem; Roger couldn't call if she didn't have a telephone. Maybe being broke had some advantages after all.

She didn't know what she'd do if Roger came down here personally to take her back to Philadelphia where she "belonged." If she'd ever "belonged" any one place, it was here, because John was here. Maybe she couldn't go to the symphony, or go skiing in Switzerland, or shopping in Paris. It didn't matter now and hadn't mattered then. All those things were nice, but unimportant. Paying bills was important. Taking care of the cattle was important.

Roger was capable of anything. Part of him was so civilized that it was truly difficult to believe he could be violent. People who'd known him all his life thought he was one of the nicest men walking the face of the earth. And he could be, but there was another part of him that flew into insanely jealous rages.

If he came down here, if she had to see him again...if he touched her in even the smallest way...she knew she couldn't handle it.

The last time had been the worst.

His parents had been in Europe. Roger had accepted an invitation for them to attend a dinner party with a few of his business associates and clients. Michelle had been extremely careful all during the evening not to say or do anything that could be considered flirtatious, but it hadn't been enough. On the way home, Roger had started the familiar catechism: She'd smiled a lot at Mr. So-and-So; had he propositioned her? He had, hadn't he? Why didn't she just admit it? He'd seen the looks passing between them.

By the time they'd arrived home, Michelle had been braced to run, if necessary, but Roger had settled down in the den to brood. She'd gone to bed, so worn out from mingled tension and relief that she'd drifted to sleep almost immediately.

Then, suddenly, the light had gone on and he'd been there, his face twisted with rage as he yelled at her. Terrified, screaming, stunned by being jerked from a sound sleep, she'd fought him when he jerked her half off the bed and began tearing at her nightgown, but she'd been helpless against him. He'd stripped the gown away and begun lashing at her with his belt, the buckle biting into her flesh again and again.

By the time he'd quit, she had been covered with raw welts and a multitude of small, bleeding cuts from the buckle, and she'd screamed so much she could no longer make a sound. Her eyes had been almost swollen shut from crying. She could still remember the silence as he'd stood there by the bed, breathing hard as he looked down at her. Then he'd fallen on his knees, burying his face in her tangled hair. "I love you so much," he'd said.

That night, while he'd slept, she had crept out and taken a cab to a hospital emergency room. Two years had passed, but the small white scars were still visible on her back, buttocks and upper thighs. They would fade with time, becoming impossible to see, but the scar left on her mind by the sheer terror of that night hadn't faded at all. The demons she feared all wore Roger's face.

But now she couldn't run from him; she had no other place to go, no other place where she wanted to be. She was legally free of him now, and there was nothing he could do to make her return. Legally she could stop him from calling her. He was harassing her; she could get a court order prohibiting him from contacting her in any way.

But she wouldn't, unless he forced her to it. She opened her eyes and stared at herself again. Oh, it was classic. A counselor at the hospital had even talked with her about it. She didn't want anyone to know her husband had abused her; it would be humiliating, as if it were somehow her fault. She didn't want people to pity her, she didn't want them to talk about her, and she especially didn't want John to know. It was too ugly, and she felt ashamed.

Suddenly she felt the walls closing in on her, stifling her. She had to get out and *do* something, or she might begin crying, and she didn't want that to happen. If she started crying now, she wouldn't be able to stop.

She got in the old truck and drove around the pastures, looking at the new sections of fence John's men had put up. They had finished and returned to their regular chores. Tomorrow they'd ride over on horseback and move the herd to this pasture with its high, thick growth of grass. The cattle could get their fill without walking so much, and they'd gain weight.

As she neared the house again she noticed how high the grass and weeds had gotten in the yard. It was so bad she might need to move the herd to the yard to graze instead of to the pasture. Yard work had come in a poor second to all the other things that had needed doing, but now, thanks to John, she had both the time and energy to do something about it.

She got out the lawnmower and pushed it up and down the yard, struggling to force it through the high grass. Little green mounds piled up in neat rows behind her. When that was finished, she took a knife from the kitchen and hacked down the weeds that had grown up next to the house. The physical activity acted like a sedative, blunting the edge of fear and finally abolishing it altogether. She didn't have any reason to be afraid; Roger wasn't going to do anything.

Subconsciously she dreaded going to bed that night, wondering if she would spend the night dozing, only to jerk awake every few moments, her heart pounding with fear as she waited for her particular demon to leap screaming out of the darkness and drag her out of bed. She didn't want to let Roger have that kind of power over her, but memories of that night still nagged at the edges of her mind. Someday she would be free of him. She swore it; she promised it to herself.

When she finally went reluctantly up the stairs and paused in the doorway to her delicately feminine room, she was overcome by a wave of memories that made her shake. She hadn't expected this reaction; she'd been thinking of Roger, but it was John who dominated this room. Roger had never set foot in here. John had slept sprawled in that bed. John had showered in that bathroom. The room was filled with his presence.

She had lain beneath him on that bed, twisting and straining with a pleasure so intense that she'd been mindless with it. She remembered the taut, savage look on his face, the gentleness of his hands as he restrained his strength which could too easily bruise a woman's soft skin. Her body tingled as she remembered the way he'd touched her, the places he'd touched her.

Then she realized that John had given her more than pleasure. She hadn't been aware of fearing men, but on some deep level of her mind, she had. In the two years since her divorce she hadn't been out on a date, and she'd managed to disguise the truth from herself by being part of a crowd that included men. Because she'd laughed with them, skied and swam with them— as long as it was a group activity, but never *alone* with a man—she'd been able to tell herself that Roger hadn't warped her so badly after all. She was strong; she could put all that behind her and not blame all men for what one man had done.

She hadn't blamed them, but she'd feared their strength. Though she'd never gone into a panic if a man touched her casually, she hadn't liked it and had always retreated.

Perhaps it would have been that way with John, too, if her long obsession with him hadn't predisposed her to accept his touch. But she'd yearned for him for so long, like a child crying for the moon, that her hunger had overcome her instinctive reluctance.

And he'd been tender, careful, generous in the giving of pleasure. In the future his passion might become rougher, but a bond of physical trust had been forged during the night that would never be broken.

Not once was her sleep disturbed by nightmares of Roger. Even in sleep, she felt John's arms around her.

Chapter 6

She had half expected John to be among the men who rode over the next morning to move the cattle to the east pasture, and a sharp pang of disappointment went through her as she realized he hadn't come. Then enthusiasm overrode her disappointment as she ran out to meet them. She'd never been in on an actual "cattle drive," short as it was, and was as excited as a child, her face glowing when she skidded to a stop in front of the mounted men.

"I want to help," she announced, green eyes sparkling in the early morning sun. The respite from the hard physical work she'd been doing made her feel like doing cartwheels on the lawn. She hadn't realized how tired she'd been until she'd had the opportunity to rest, but now she was bubbling over with energy.

Nev Luther, John's lanky and laconic foreman, looked down at her with consternation written across his weathered face. The boss had been explicit in his instructions that Michelle was not to be allowed to work in any way, which was a damned odd position for him to take. Nev couldn't remember the boss ever wanting anyone *not* to work. But orders were orders, and folks who valued their hides didn't ignore the boss's orders.

Not that he'd expected any trouble doing what he'd been told. Somehow he just hadn't pictured fancy Michelle Cabot doing any ranch work, let alone jumping up and down with joy at the prospect. Now what was he going to do? He cleared his throat, reluctant to do anything that would wipe the glowing smile off her face, but even more reluctant to get in trouble with Rafferty.

Inspiration struck, and he looked around. "You got a horse?" He knew she didn't, so he figured that was a detail she couldn't get around.

Her bright face dimmed, then lit again. "I'll drive the truck," she said, and raced toward the barn. Thunderstruck, Nev watched her go, and the men with him muttered warning comments.

Now what? He couldn't haul her out of the truck and order her to stay here. He didn't think she would take orders too well, and he also had the distinct idea the boss was feeling kinda possessive about her. Nev worked with animals, so he tended to put his thoughts in animal terms. One stallion didn't allow another near his mare, and the possessive mating instinct was still alive and well in humans. Nope, he wasn't going to manhandle that woman and have Rafferty take his head off for touching her. Given the choice, he'd rather have the boss mad about his orders not being followed than in a rage because someone had touched his woman, maybe upset her and made her cry.

The stray thought that she might cry decided him in a hurry. Like most men who didn't have a lot of contact with women, he went into a panic at the thought of tears. Rafferty could just go to hell. As far as Nev was concerned, Michelle could do whatever she wanted.

Having the burden of doing everything lifted off her shoulders made all the difference in the world. Michelle enjoyed the sunshine, the lowing of the cattle as they protested the movement, the tight-knit way the cowboys and their horses worked together. She bumped along the pasture in the old truck, which wasn't much good for rounding up strays but could keep the herd nudging forward. The only problem was, riding—or driving—drag was the dustiest place to be.

It wasn't long before one of the cowboys gallantly offered to drive the truck and give her a break from the dust. She took his horse without a qualm. She loved riding; at first it had been the only thing about ranch life that she'd enjoyed. She quickly found that riding a horse for pleasure was a lot different from riding a trained cutting horse. The horse didn't wait for her to tell it what to do. When a cow broke for freedom, the horse broke with it, and Michelle had to learn to go with the movement. She soon got the hang of it though, and before long she was almost hoping a stray would bolt, just for the joy of riding the quick-moving animal.

Nev swore long and eloquently under his breath when he saw the big gray coming across the pasture. Damn, the fat was in the fire now.

John was eyeing the truck with muted anger as he rode up, but there was no way the broad-shouldered figure in it was Michelle. Disbelieving, his black gaze swept the riders and lighted unerringly on the wand-slim rider with sunny hair tumbling below a hat. He reined in when he reached Nev, his jaw set as he looked at his foreman. "Well?" he asked in a dead-level voice.

Nev scratched his jaw, turning his head to watch Michelle snatch her hat off her head and wave it at a rambunctious calf. "I tried," he mumbled. He glanced back to meet John's narrowed gaze. Damned if eyes as black as hell couldn't look cold. "Hell, boss, it's her truck and her land. What was I supposed to do? Tie her down?"

"She's not in the truck," John pointed out.

"Well, it was so dusty back there that . . . ah, *hell!*"

Nev gave up trying to explain himself in disgust and spurred to head off a stray. John let him go, picking his way over to Michelle. He would take it up with Nev later, though already his anger was fading. She wasn't doing anything dangerous, even if he didn't like seeing her covered with dust.

She smiled at him when he rode up, a smile of such pure pleasure that his brows pulled together in a little frown. It was the first time he'd seen that smile since she'd been back, but until now he hadn't realized it had been missing. She looked happy. Faced with a smile like that, no wonder Nev had caved in and let her do what she wanted.

"Having fun?" he asked wryly.

"Yes, I am." Her look dared him to make something of it.

"I had a call from the lawyer this morning. He'll have everything ready for us to sign the day after to-morrow."

"That's good." Her ranch would shrink by a sizable hunk of acreage, but at least it would be clear of any large debt.

He watched her for a minute, leaning his forearms on the saddle horn. "Want to ride back to the house with me?"

"For a quickie?" she asked tartly, her green eyes beginning to spit fire at him.

His gaze drifted to her breasts. "I was thinking more of a slowie."

"So your men would have even more to gossip about?"

He drew a deep, irritated breath. "I suppose you want me to sneak over in the dead of night. We're not teenagers, damn it."

"No, we're not," she agreed. Then she said abruptly, "I'm not pregnant."

He didn't know if he should feel relieved, or irritated that this news meant it would be several days before she'd let him make love to her again. He wanted to curse, already feeling frustrated. Instead he said, "At least we didn't have to wait a couple of weeks, wondering."

"No, we didn't." She had known that the timing made it unlikely she'd conceive, but she'd still felt a small pang of regret that morning. Common sense aside, there was a deeply primitive part of her that wondered what woman wouldn't want to have his baby. He was so intensely masculine that he made other men pale in comparison, like a blooded stallion matched against scrub stock.

The gray shifted restively beneath him, and John controlled the big animal with his legs. "Actually, I don't have time, even for a quickie. I came to give Nev some instructions, then stop by the house to let you know where I'll be. I have to fly to Miami this afternoon, and I may not be back for a couple of days. If I'm not, drive to Tampa by yourself and sign those papers, and I'll detour on my way back to sign them."

Michelle twisted in the saddle to look at the battered, rusting old truck bouncing along behind the cattle. There was no way she would trust that relic to take her any place she couldn't get back from on foot. "I think I'll wait until you're back."

"Use the Mercedes. Just call the ranch and Nev will have a couple of men bring it over. I wouldn't trust that piece of junk you've been driving to get you to the grocery store and back."

It could have been a gesture between friends, a neighborly loan of a car, even something a lover might do, but Michelle sensed that John intended it to mean more than that. He was maneuvering her into his home as his mistress, and if she accepted the loan of the car, she would be just that much more dependent on him. Yet she was almost cornered into accepting because she had no other way of getting to Tampa, and her own sense of duty insisted that she sign those papers as soon as possible, to clear the debt.

He was waiting for her answer, and finally she couldn't hesitate any longer. "All right." Her surrender was quiet, almost inaudible.

He hadn't realized how tense he'd been until his muscles relaxed. The thought that she might try driving to Tampa in that old wreck had been worrying him since he'd gotten the call from Miami. His mother had gotten herself into financial hot water again, and, distasteful as it was to him, he wouldn't let her starve.

No matter what, she was his mother. Loyalty went bone deep with him, a lot deeper than aggravation.

He'd even thought of taking Michelle with him, just to have her near. But Miami was too close to Palm Beach; too many of her old friends were there, bored, and just looking for some lark to spice up their lives. It was possible that some jerk with more money than brains would make an offer she couldn't refuse. He had to credit her with trying to make a go of the place, but she wasn't cut out for the life and must be getting tired of working so hard and getting nowhere. If someone offered to pay her fare, she might turn her back and walk away, back to the jet-set life-style she knew so well. No matter how slim the chance of it happening, any chance at all was too much for him. No way would he risk losing her now.

For the first time in his life he felt insecure about a woman. She wanted him, but was it enough to keep her with him? For the first time in his life, it was important. The hunger he felt for her was so deep that he wouldn't be satisfied until she was living under his roof and sleeping in his bed, where he could take care of her and pamper her as much as he wanted.

Yes, she wanted him. He could please her in bed; he could take care of her. But she didn't want him as much as he wanted her. She kept resisting him, trying to keep a distance between them even now, after they'd shared a night and a bed, and a joining that still shook him with its power. It seemed as if every time he tried to bring her closer, she backed away a little more.

He reached out and touched her cheek, stroking his fingertips across her skin and feeling the patrician bone structure that gave her face such an angular, haughty look. "Miss me while I'm gone," he said, his tone making it a command.

A small wry smile tugged at the corners of her wide mouth. "Okay."

"Damn it," he said mildly. "You're not going to boost my ego, are you?"

"Does it need it?"

"Where you're concerned, yeah."

"That's a little hard to believe. Is missing someone a two-way street, or will you be too busy in Miami to bother?"

"I'll be busy, but I'll bother anyway."

"Be careful." She couldn't stop the words. They were the caring words that always went before a trip, a magic incantation to keep a loved one safe. The thought of not seeing him made her feel cold and empty. Miss him? He had no idea how much, that the missing was a razor, already slashing at her insides.

He wanted to kiss her, but not with his men watching. Instead he nodded an acknowledgment and turned his horse away to rejoin Nev. The two men rode together for a time, and Michelle could see Nev give an occasional nod as he listened to John's instructions. Then John was gone, kicking the gray into a long ground-eating stride that quickly took horse and rider out of sight.

Despite the small, lost feeling she couldn't shake, Michelle didn't allow herself to brood over the next several days. There was too much going on, and even though John's men had taken over the ranching chores, there were still other chores that, being cowboys, they didn't see. If it didn't concern cattle or horses, then it didn't concern them. Now Michelle found other chores to occupy her time. She painted the porch, put up a new post for the mailbox and spent as much time as she could with the men.

The ranch seemed like a ranch again, with all the activity, dust, smells and curses filling the air. The cattle were dipped, the calves branded, the young bulls clipped. Once Michelle would have wrinkled her nose in distaste, but now she saw the activity as new signs of life, both in the ranch and in herself.

On the second day Nev drove the Mercedes over while one of the other men brought an extra horse for Nev to ride. Michelle couldn't quite look the man in the eye as she took the keys from him, but he didn't seem to see anything unusual about her driving John's car.

After driving the pickup truck for so long, the power and responsiveness of the Mercedes felt odd. She was painfully cautious on the long drive to Tampa. It was hard to imagine that she'd ever been blasé about the expensive, sporty cars she'd driven over the years, but she could remember her carelessness with the white Porsche her father had given her on her eighteenth birthday. The amount of money represented by the small white machine hadn't made any impression on her.

Everything was relative. Then, the money spent for the Porsche hadn't been much. If she had that much now, she would feel rich.

She signed the papers at the lawyer's office, then immediately made the drive back, not wanting to have the Mercedes out longer than necessary.

The rest of the week was calm, though she wished John would call to let her know when he would be back. The two days had stretched into five, and she couldn't stop the tormenting doubts that popped up in unguarded moments. Was he with another woman? Even though he was down there on business, she knew all too well how women flocked to him, and he wouldn't be working twenty-four hours a day. He hadn't made any commitments to her; he was free to take other women out if he wanted. No matter how often she repeated those words to herself, they still hurt.

But if John didn't call, at least Roger didn't, either. For a while she'd been afraid he would begin calling regularly, but the reassuring silence continued. Maybe something or someone else had taken his attention. Maybe his business concerns were taking all his time. Whatever it was, Michelle was profoundly grateful.

The men didn't come over on Friday morning. The cattle were grazing peacefully in the east pasture; all the fencing had been repaired; everything had been taken care of. Michelle put a load of clothing in the washer, then spent the morning cutting the grass again. She was soaked with sweat when she went inside at noon to make a sandwich for lunch.

It was oddly silent in the house, or maybe it was just silent in comparison to the roar of the lawnmower. She needed water. Breathing hard, she turned on the faucet to let the water get cold while she got a glass from the cabinet, but only a trickle of water ran out, then stopped altogether. Frowning, Michelle turned the faucet off, then on again. Nothing happened. She tried the hot water. Nothing.

Groaning, she leaned against the sink. That was just what she needed, for the water pump to break down.

It took only a few seconds for the silence of the house to connect with the lack of water, and she slowly straightened. Reluctantly she reached for the light switch and flicked it on. Nothing.

The electricity had been cut off.

That was why it was so quiet. The refrigerator wasn't humming; the clocks weren't ticking; the ceiling fan was still.

Breathing raggedly, she sank into a chair. She had forgotten the last notice. She had put it in a drawer and forgotten it, distracted by John and the sudden activity around the ranch. Not that any excuse was worth a hill of beans, she reminded herself. Not that she'd had the money to pay the bill even if she had remembered it.

She had to be practical. People had lived for thousands of years without electricity, so she could, too. Cooking was out; the range top, built-in oven and microwave were all electric, but she wasn't the world's best cook anyway, so that wasn't critical. She could eat without cooking. The refrigerator was empty except for milk and some odds and ends. Thinking about the milk reminded her how thirsty she was, so she poured a glass of the cold milk and swiftly returned the carton to the refrigerator.

There was a kerosene lamp and a supply of candles in the pantry, so she would have light. The most critical item was water. She had to have water to drink and bathe. At least the cattle could drink from the shallow creek that snaked across the east pasture, so she wouldn't have to worry about them.

There was an old well about a hundred yards behind the house, but she didn't know if it had gone dry or simply been covered when the other well had been drilled. Even if the well was still good, how would she get the water up? There was a rope in the barn, but she didn't have a bucket.

She did have seventeen dollars, though, the last of her cash. If the well had water in it, she'd coax the old truck down to the hardware store and buy a water bucket.

She got a rope from the barn, a pan from the kitchen and trudged the hundred yards to the old well. It was almost overgrown with weeds and vines that she had to clear away while keeping an uneasy eye out for snakes. Then she tugged the heavy wooden cover to the side and dropped the pan into the well, letting the rope slip lightly through her hands. It wasn't a deep well; in only a second or two there was a distinct splash, and she began hauling the pan back up. When she got it to the top, a half cup of clear water was still in the pan despite the banging it had received, and Michelle sighed with relief. Now all she had to do was get the bucket.

By the time dusk fell, she was convinced that the pioneers had all been as muscular as the Incredible Hulk; every muscle in her body ached. She had drawn a bucket of water and walked the distance back to the house so many times she didn't want to think about it. The electricity had been cut off while the washer had been in the middle of its cycle, so she had to rinse the clothes out by hand and hang them to dry. She had to have water to drink. She had to have water to bathe. She had to have water to flush the toilet. Modern conveniences were damned *in*convenient without electricity.

But at least she was too tired to stay up long and waste the candles. She set a candle in a saucer on the bedside table, with matches alongside in case she woke up during the night. She was asleep almost as soon as she stretched out between the sheets.

The next morning she ate a peanut butter and jelly sandwich for breakfast, then cleaned out the refrigerator, so she wouldn't have to smell spoiled food. The house was oddly oppressive, as if the life had gone out of it, so she spent most of the day outdoors, watching the cattle graze, and thinking.

She would have to sell the beef cattle now, rather than wait to fatten them on grain. She wouldn't get as much for them, but she had to have money *now*. It had been foolish of her to let things go this far. Pride had kept her from asking for John's advice and help in arranging the sale; now she had to ask him. He would know who to contact and how to transport the cattle. The money would keep her going, allow her to care for the remainder of the herd until spring, when she would have more beef ready to sell. Pride was one thing, but she had carried it to the point of stupidity.

Still, if this had happened ten days earlier she wouldn't even have considered asking John's advice. She had been so completely isolated from human trust that any overture would have made her back away, rather than entice her closer. But John hadn't let her back away; he'd come after her, taken care of things over her protests, and very gently, thoroughly seduced her. A seed of trust had been sown that was timidly growing, though it frightened her to think of relying on someone else, even for good advice.

It was sultry that night, the air thick with humidity. The heat added by the candles and kerosene lamp made it unbearable inside, and though she bathed in the cool water she had hauled from the well, she immediately felt sticky again. It was too early and too hot to sleep, so finally she went out on the porch in search of a breeze.

She curled up in a wicker chair padded with overstuffed cushions, sighing in relief as a breath of wind fanned her face. The night sounds of crickets and frogs surrounded her with a hypnotic lullaby, and before long her eyelids were drooping. She never quite dozed, but sank into a peaceful lethargy where time passed unnoticed. It might have been two hours or half an hour later when she was disturbed by the sound of a motor and the crunching of tires on gravel; headlights flashed into her eyes just as she opened them, making her flinch and turn her face from the blinding light. Then the lights were killed and the motor silenced. She sat up straighter, her heart beginning to pound as a tall, broad-shouldered man got out of the truck and slammed the door. The starlight wasn't bright, but she didn't need light to identify him when every cell in her body tingled with awareness.

Despite his boots, he didn't make a lot of noise as he came up the steps. "John," she murmured, her voice only a low whisper of sound, but he felt the vibration and turned toward her chair.

She was completely awake now, and becoming indignant. "Why didn't you call? I waited to hear from you—"

"I don't like telephones," he muttered as he walked toward her. That was only part of the reason. Talking to her on the telephone would only have made him want her more, and his nights had been pure hell as it was.

"That isn't much of an excuse."

"It'll do," he drawled. "What are you doing out here? The house is so dark I thought you must have gone to bed early."

Which wouldn't have stopped him from waking her, she thought wryly. "It's too hot to sleep."

He grunted in agreement, bending down to slide his arms under her legs and shoulders. Startled, Michelle grabbed his neck with both arms as he lifted her, then took her place in the chair and settled her on his lap. An almost painful sense of relief filled her as his nearness eased tension she hadn't even been aware of feeling. She was surrounded by his strength and warmth, and the subtle male scent of his skin reaffirmed the sense of homecoming, of rightness. Bonelessly she melted against him, lifting her mouth to his.

The kiss was long and hot, his lips almost bruising hers in his need, but she didn't mind, because her own need was just as urgent. His hands slipped under the light nightgown that was all she wore, finding her soft and naked, and a shudder wracked his body.

He muttered a soft curse. "Sweet hell, woman, you were sitting out here practically naked."

"No one else is around to see." She said the words against his throat, her lips moving over his hard flesh and finding the vibrant hollow where his pulse throbbed.

Heat and desire wrapped around them, sugar-sweet and mindless. From the moment he touched her, she'd wanted only to lie down with him and sink into the textures and sensations of lovemaking. She twisted in his arms, trying to press her breasts fully against him and whimpering a protest as he prevented her from moving.

"This won't work," he said, securing his hold on her and getting to his feet with her still in his arms. "We'd better find a bed, because this chair won't hold up to what I have in mind."

He carried her inside, and as he had done before, he flipped the switch for the light in the entry, so he would be able to see while going up the stairs. He paused when the light didn't come on. "You've got a blown bulb."

Tension invaded her body again. "The power's off."

He gave a low laugh. "Well, hell. Do you have a flashlight? The last thing I want to do right now is trip on the stairs and break our necks."

"There's a kerosene lamp on the table." She wriggled in his arms, and he slowly let her slide to the floor, reluctant to let her go even for a moment. She fumbled for the matches and struck one, the bright glow guiding her hands as she removed the glass chimney and held the flame to the wick. It caught, and the light grew when she put the chimney back in place.

John took the lamp in his left hand, folding her close to his side with his other arm as they started up the stairs. "Have you called the power company to report it?"

She had to laugh. "They know."

"How long will it take them to get it back on?"

Well, he might as well know now. Sighing, she admitted, "The electricity's been cut off. I couldn't pay the bill."

He stopped, his brows drawing together in increasing temper as he turned. "Damn it to hell! How long has it been off?"

"Since yesterday morning."

He exhaled through his clenched teeth, making a hissing sound. "You've been here without water and lights for a day and a half? Of all the damned stubborn stunts... Why in hell didn't you give the bill to me?" He yelled the last few words at her, his eyes snapping black fury in the yellow light from the lamp.

"I don't want you paying my bills!" she snapped, pulling away from him.

"Well, that's just tough!" Swearing under his breath, he caught her hand and pulled her up the stairs, then into her bedroom. He set the lamp on the bedside table and crossed to the closet, opened the doors and began pulling her suitcases from the top shelf.

"What are you doing?" she cried, wrenching the suitcase from him.

He lifted another case down. "Packing your things," he replied shortly. "If you don't want to help, just sit on the bed and stay out of the way."

"Stop it!" She tried to prevent him from taking an armful of clothes from the closet, but he merely sidestepped her and tossed the clothes onto the bed, then returned to the closet for another armful.

"You're going with me," he said, his voice steely. "This is Saturday; it'll be Monday before I can take care of the bill. There's no way in hell I'm going to leave you here. God Almighty, you don't even have water!"

Michelle pushed her hair from her eyes. "I have water. I've been drawing it from the old well."

He began swearing again and turned from the closet to the dresser. Before she could say anything her underwear was added to the growing pile on the bed. "I can't stay with you," she said desperately, knowing events were already far out of her control. "You know how it'll look! I can manage another couple of days—"

"I don't give a damn how it looks!" he snapped. "And just so you understand me, I'm going to give it to you in plain English. You're going with me now, and you won't be coming back. This isn't a two-day visit. I'm tired of worrying about you out here all by yourself; this is the last straw. You're too damned proud to tell me when you need help, so I'm going to take over and handle everything, the way I should have in the beginning."

Michelle shivered, staring at him. It was true that she shrank from the gossip she knew would run through the county like wildfire, but that wasn't the main reason for her reluctance. Living with him would destroy the last fragile buffers she had retained against being overwhelmed by him in every respect. She wouldn't be able to keep any emotional distance as a safety precaution, just as physical distance would be impossible. She would be in his home, in his bed, eating his food, totally dependent on him.

It frightened her so much that she found herself backing away from him, as if by increasing the distance between them she could weaken his force and fury. "I've been getting by without you," she whispered.

"Is this what you call 'getting by'?" he shouted, slinging the contents of another drawer onto the bed. "You were working yourself half to death, and you're damned lucky you weren't hurt trying to do a two-man job! You don't have any money. You don't have a safe car to drive. You probably don't have enough to eat—and now you don't have electricity."

"I know what I don't have!"

"Well, I'll tell you something else you don't have: a choice. You're going. Now get dressed."

She stood against the wall on the other side of the room, very still and straight. When she didn't move his head jerked up, but something about her made his mouth soften. She looked defiant and stubborn, but her eyes were frightened, and she looked so frail it was like a punch in the gut, staggering him.

He crossed the room with quick strides and hauled her into his arms, folding her against him as if he couldn't tolerate another minute of not touching her. He buried his face in her hair, wanting to sweep her up and keep her from ever being frightened again. "I won't let you do it," he muttered in a raspy voice. "You're trying to keep me at a distance, and I'll be damned if I'll let you do it. Does it matter so much if people know about us? Are you ashamed because I'm not a member of your jet set?"

She gave a shaky laugh, her fingers digging into his back. "Of course not. *I'm* not one of the jet set." How could any woman ever be ashamed of him?

His lips brushed her forehead, leaving warmth behind. "Then what is it?"

She bit her lip, her mind whirling with images of the past and fears of the future. "The summer I was nineteen...you called me a parasite." She had never forgotten the words or the deep hurt they'd caused, and an echo of it was in her low, drifting voice. "You were right."

"Wrong," he whispered, winding his fingers through the strands of her bright hair. "A parasite doesn't give anything, it only takes. I didn't understand, or maybe I was jealous because I wanted it all.

I have it all now, and I won't give it up. I've waited ten years for you, baby; I'm not going to settle for half measures now."

He tilted her head back, and his mouth closed warmly, hungrily, over hers, overwhelming any further protests. With a little sigh Michelle gave in, going up on her tiptoes to press herself against him. Regrets could wait; if this were all she would have of heaven, she was going to grab it with both hands. He would probably decide that she'd given in so she could have an easier life, but maybe that was safer than for him to know she was head over heels in love with him.

She slipped out of his arms and quietly changed into jeans and a silk tunic, then set about restoring order out of the chaos he'd made of her clothes. Traveling had taught her to be a fast, efficient packer. As she finished each case, he carried it out to the truck. Finally only her makeup and toiletries were left.

"We'll come back tomorrow for anything else you want," he promised, holding the lamp for the last trip down the stairs. When she stepped outside he extinguished the lamp and placed it on the table, then followed her and locked the door behind him.

"What will your housekeeper think?" she blurted nervously as she got in the truck. It hurt to be leaving her home. She had hidden herself away here, sinking deep roots into the ranch. She had found peace and healing in the hard work.

"That I should have called to let her know when I'd be home," he said, laughing as relief and anticipation filled him. "I came here straight from the airport. My bag is in back with yours." He couldn't wait to get home, to see Michelle's clothing hanging next to his in the closet, to have her toiletries in his bathroom, to sleep with her every night in his bed. He'd never before wanted to live with a woman, but with Michelle it felt necessary. There was no way he would ever feel content with less than everything she had to give.

Chapter 7

It was midmorning when Michelle woke, and she lay there for a moment alone in the big bed, trying to adjust to the change. She was in John's house, in his bed. He had gotten up hours ago, before dawn, and left her with a kiss on the forehead and an order to catch up on her sleep. She stretched, becoming aware of both her nakedness and the ache in her muscles. She didn't want to move, didn't want to leave the comforting cocoon of sheets and pillows that carried John's scent. The memory of shattering pleasure made her body tingle, and she moved restlessly. He hadn't slept much, hadn't let her sleep until he'd finally left the bed to go about his normal day's work.

If only he had taken her with him. She felt awkward with Edie, the housekeeper. What must she be thinking? They had met only briefly, because John had ushered Michelle upstairs with blatantly indecent haste, but her impression had been of height, dignity and cool control. The housekeeper wouldn't say anything if she disapproved, but then, she wouldn't have to; Michelle would know.

Finally she got out of bed and showered, smiling wryly to herself as she realized she wouldn't have to skimp on hot water. Central air-conditioning kept the house comfortably cool, which was another comfort she had given up in an effort to reduce the bills. No matter what her mental state, she would be physically comfortable here. It struck her as odd that she'd never been to John's house before; she'd had no idea what to expect. Perhaps another old ranch house like hers, though her father had remodeled and modernized it completely on the inside before they had moved in, and it was in fact as luxurious as the home she had been used to. But John's house was Spanish in style, and was only eight years old. The cool adobe-colored brick and high ceilings kept the heat at bay, and a colorful array of houseplants brought freshness to the air. She'd been surprised at the greenery, then decided that the plants were Edie's doing. The U-shaped house wrapped around a pool landscaped to the point that it resembled a jungle lagoon more than a pool, and every room had a view of the pool and patio.

She had been surprised at the luxury. John was a long way from poor, but the house had cost a lot of money that he would normally have plowed back into the ranch. She had expected something more utilitarian, but at the same time it was very much his *home*. His presence permeated it, and everything was arranged for his comfort.

Finally she forced herself to stop hesitating and go downstairs; if Edie intended to be hostile, she might as well know now.

The layout of the house was simple, and she found the kitchen without any problem. All she had to do was follow her nose to the coffee. As she entered, Edie looked around, her face expressionless, and Michelle's heart sank. Then the housekeeper planted her hands on her hips and said calmly, "I told John it was about damned time he got a woman in this house."

Relief flooded through Michelle, because something in her would have shriveled if Edie had looked at her with contempt. She was much more sensitive to what other people thought now than she had been when she was younger and had the natural arrogance of youth. Life had defeated that arrogance and taught her not to expect roses.

Faint color rushed to her cheeks. "John didn't make much of an effort to introduce us last night. I'm Michelle Cabot."

"Edie Ward. Are you ready for breakfast? I'm the cook, too."

"I'll wait until lunch, thank you. Does John come back for lunch?" It embarrassed her to have to ask.

"If he's working close by. How about coffee?"

"I can get it," Michelle said quickly. "Where are the cups?"

Edie opened the cabinet to the left of the sink and got down a cup, handing it to Michelle. "It'll be nice to have company here during the day," she said. "These damn cowhands aren't much for talking."

Whatever Michelle had expected, Edie didn't conform. She had to be fifty; though her hair was still dark, there was something about her that made her look her age. She was tall and broad shouldered, with the erect carriage of a Mother Superior and the same sort of unflappable dignity, but she also had the wise, slightly weary eyes of someone who has been around the block a few times too many. Her quiet acceptance made Michelle relax; Edie didn't pass judgments.

But for all the easing of tension, Edie quietly and firmly discouraged Michelle from helping with any of the household chores. "Rafferty would have both our heads," she said. "Housework is what he pays me to do, and around here we try not to rile him."

So Michelle wandered around the house, poking her head into every room and wondering how long she would be able to stand the boredom and emptiness. Working the ranch by herself had been so hard that she had sometimes wanted nothing more than to collapse where she stood, but there had always been a purpose to the hours. She liked ranching. It wasn't easy, but it suited her far better than the dual roles of ornament and mistress. This lack of purpose made her uneasy. She had hoped living with John would mean doing things with him, sharing the work and the worries with him . . . just as married couples did.

She sucked in her breath at the thought; she was in his—still *his*—bedroom at the time, standing in front of the open closet staring at his clothes, as if the sight of his personal possessions would bring him closer. Slowly she reached out and fingered a shirt sleeve. Her clothes were in the closet beside his, but she didn't belong. This was his house, his bedroom, his closet, and she was merely another possession, to be enjoyed in bed but forgotten at sunrise. Wryly she admitted that it was better than nothing; no matter what the cost to her pride, she would stay here as long as he wanted her, because she was so sick with love for him that she'd take anything she could get. But what she wanted, what she really wanted more than anything in her life, was to have his love as well as his desire. She wanted to marry him, to be his partner, his friend as well as his lover, to belong here as much as he did.

Part of her was startled that she could think of marriage again, even with John. Roger had destroyed her trust, her optimism about life; at least, she'd thought he had. Trust had already bloomed again, a fragile phoenix poking its head up from the ashes. For the first time she recognized her own resilience; she had been altered by the terror and shame of her marriage, but not destroyed. She was healing, and most of it was because of John. She had loved him for so long that her love seemed like the only continuous thread of her life, always there, somehow giving her something to hold on to even when she'd thought it didn't matter.

At last restlessness drove her from the house. She was reluctant to even ask questions, not wanting to interfere with anyone's work, but she decided to walk around and look at everything. There was a world of difference between John's ranch and hers. Here everything was neat and well-maintained, with fresh paint on the barns and fences, the machinery humming. Healthy, spirited horses pranced in the corral or grazed in the pasture. The supply shed was in better shape than her barn. Her ranch had once looked like this, and determination filled her that it would again.

Who was looking after her cattle? She hadn't asked John, not that she'd been given a chance to ask him anything. He'd had her in bed so fast that she hadn't had time to think; then he'd left while she was still dozing.

By the time John came home at dusk, Michelle was so on edge that she could feel her muscles twitching with tension. As soon as he came in from the kitchen his eyes swept the room, and hard satisfaction crossed his face when he saw her. All day long he'd been fighting the urge to come back to the house, picturing her here, under his roof at last. Even when he'd built the house, eight years before, he'd wondered what *she* would think of it, if she'd like it, how she would look in these rooms. It wasn't a grand mansion like those in Palm Beach, but it had been custom built to his specifications for comfort, beauty and a certain level of luxury.

She looked as fresh and perfect as early-morning sunshine, while he was covered with sweat and dust, his jaw dark with a day's growth of beard. If he touched her now, he'd leave dirty prints on her creamy white dress, and he had to touch her soon or go crazy. "Come on up with me," he growled, his boots ringing on the flagstone floor as he went to the stairs.

Michelle followed him at a slower pace, wondering if he already regretted bringing her here. He hadn't kissed her, or even smiled.

He was stripping off his shirt by the time she entered the bedroom, and he carelessly dropped the dirty, sweat-stained garment on the carpet. She shivered in response at the sight of his broad, hair-covered chest and powerful shoulders, her pulse throbbing as she remembered how it felt when he moved over her and slowly let her take his weight, nestling her breasts into that curly hair.

"What've you been doing today?" he asked as he went into the bathroom.

"Nothing," Michelle answered with rueful truthfulness, shaking away the sensual lethargy that had been stealing over her.

Splashing sounds came from the bathroom, and when he reappeared a few minutes later his face was clean of the dust that had covered it before. Damp strands of black hair curled at his temples. He looked at her, and an impatient scowl darkened his face. Bending down, he pried his boots off, then began unbuckling his belt.

Her heart began pounding again. He was going to take her to bed right now, and she wouldn't have a chance to talk to him if she didn't do it before he reached for her. Nervously she picked up his dirty boots to put them in the closet, wondering how to start. "Wait," she blurted. "I need to talk to you."

He didn't see any reason to wait. "So talk," he said, unzipping his jeans and pushing them down his thighs.

She inhaled deeply. "I've been bored with nothing to do all day—"

John straightened, his eyes hardening as she broke off. Hell, he should have expected it. When you acquired something expensive, you had to pay for its upkeep. "All right," he said in an even tone. "I'll give you the keys to the Mercedes, and tomorrow I'll open a checking account for you."

She froze as the meaning of his words seared through her, and all the color washed out of her face. No. There was no way she'd let him turn her into a pet, a chirpy sexual toy, content with a fancy car and charge accounts. Fury rose in her like an inexorable wave, rushing up and bursting out of control. Fiercely she hurled the boots at him; startled, he dodged the first one, but the second one hit him in the chest. "What the hell—"

"No!" she shouted, her eyes like green fire in a face gone curiously pale. She was standing rigidly, her fists clenched at her sides. "I don't want your money or your damned car! I want to take care of my cattle and my ranch, not be left here every day like some fancy...*sex doll*, waiting for you to get home and play with me!"

He kicked his jeans away, leaving him clad only in his briefs. His own temper was rising, but he clamped it under control. That control was evident in his quiet, level voice. "I don't think of you as a sex doll. What brought that on?"

She was white and shaking. "You brought me straight up here and started undressing."

His brows rose. "Because I was dirty from head to foot. I couldn't even kiss you without getting you dirty, and I didn't want to ruin your dress."

Her lips trembled as she looked down at the dress. "It's just a dress," she said, turning away. "It'll wash. And I'd rather be dirty myself than just left here every day with nothing to do."

"We've been over this before, and it's settled." He walked up behind her and put his hands on her shoulders, gently squeezing. "You can't handle the work; you'd only hurt yourself. Some women can do it, but you're not strong enough. Look at your wrist," he said, sliding his hand down her arm and grasping her wrist to lift it. "Your bones are too little."

Somehow she found herself leaning against him, her head resting in the hollow of his shoulder. "Stop trying to make me feel so useless!" she cried desperately. "At least let me go with you. I can chase strays—"

He turned her in his arms, crushing her against him and cutting off her words. "God, baby," he muttered. "I'm trying to protect you, not make you feel useless. It made me sick when I saw you putting up that fence, knowing what could happen if the wire lashed back on you. You could be thrown, or gored—''

"So could you."

"Not as easily. Admit it; strength counts out there. I want you safe."

It was a battle they'd already fought more times than she could remember, and nothing budged him. But she couldn't give up, because she couldn't stand many more days like today had been. "Could you stand it if you had nothing to do? If you had to just stand around and watch everybody else? Edie won't even let me help!"

"She'd damned well better not."

"See what I mean? Am I supposed to just sit all day?"

"All right, you've made your point," he said in a low voice. He'd thought she'd enjoy living a life of leisure again, but instead she'd been wound to the breaking point. He rubbed her back soothingly, and gradually she relaxed against him, her arms sliding up to hook around his neck. He'd have to find something to keep her occupied, but right now he was at a loss. It was hard to think when she was lying against him like warm silk, her firm breasts pushing into him and the sweet scent of woman rising to his nostrils. She hadn't been far from his mind all day, the thought of her pulling at him like a magnet. No matter how often he took her, the need came back even stronger than before.

Reluctantly he moved her a few inches away from him. "Dinner will be ready in about ten minutes, and I need a shower. I smell like a horse."

The hot, earthy scents of sweat, sun, leather and man didn't offend her. She found herself drawn back to him; she pressed her face into his chest, her tongue flicking out to lick daintily at his hot skin. He shuddered, all thoughts of a shower gone from his mind. Sliding his fingers into the shiny, pale gold curtain of her hair, he turned her face up and took the kiss he'd been wanting for hours.

She couldn't limit her response to him; whenever he reached for her, she was instantly his, melting into him, opening her mouth for him, ready to give as little or as much as he wanted to take. Loving him went beyond the boundaries she had known before, taking her into emotional and physical territory that was new to her. It was his control, not hers, that prevented him from tumbling her onto the bed right then. "Shower," he muttered, lifting his head. His voice was strained. "Then dinner. Then I have to do some paperwork, damn it, and it can't wait."

Michelle sensed that he expected her to object and demand his company, but more than anyone she understood about chores that couldn't be postponed. She drew back from his arms, giving him a smile. "I'm starving, so hurry up with your shower." An idea was forming in the back of her mind, one she needed to explore.

She was oddly relaxed during dinner; it somehow seemed natural to be here with him, as if the world had suddenly settled into the natural order of things. The awkwardness of the morning was gone, perhaps because of John's presence. Edie ate with them, an informality that Michelle liked. It also gave her a chance to think, because Edie's comments filled the silence and made it less apparent.

After dinner, John gave Michelle a quick kiss and a pat on the bottom. "I'll finish as fast as I can. Can you entertain yourself for a while?"

Swift irritation made up her mind for her. "I'm coming with you."

He sighed, looking down at her. "Baby, I won't get any work done at all if you're in there with me."

She gave him a withering look. "You're the biggest chauvinist walking, John Rafferty. You're going to work, all right, because you're going to show me what you're doing, and then I'm taking over your book-work."

He looked suddenly wary. "I'm not a chauvinist."

He didn't want her touching his books, either. He might as well have said it out loud, because she read his thoughts in his expression. "You can either give me something to do, or I'm going back to my house right now," she said flatly, facing him with her hands on her hips.

"Just what do you know about keeping books?"

"I minored in business administration." Let him chew on that for a while. Since he obviously wasn't going to willingly let her in his office, she stepped around him and walked down the hall without him.

"Michelle, damn it," he muttered irritably, follow-ing her.

"Just what's wrong with my doing the books?" she demanded, taking a seat at the big desk.

"I didn't bring you here to work. I want to take care of you."

"Am I going to get hurt in here? Is a pencil too heavy for me to lift?"

He scowled down at her, itching to lift her out of her chair. But her green eyes were glittering at him, and her chin had that stubborn tilt to it, showing she was ready to fight. If he pushed her, she really might go back to that dark, empty house. He could keep her here by force, but he didn't want it that way. He wanted her sweet and willing, not clawing at him like a wildcat. Hell, at least this was safer than riding herd. He'd double-check the books at night.

"All right," he growled.

Her green eyes mocked him. "You're so gracious."

"You're full of sass tonight," he mused, sitting down. "Maybe I should have made love to you before dinner after all, worked some of that out."

"Like I said, the world's biggest chauvinist." She gave him her haughty look, the one that had always made him see red before. She was beginning to enjoy baiting him.

His face darkened but he controlled himself, reaching for the pile of invoices, receipts and notes. "Pay attention, and don't screw this up," he snapped. "Taxes are bad enough without an amateur bookkeeper fouling up the records."

"I've been doing the books since Dad died," she snapped in return.

"From the looks of the place, honey, that's not much of a recommendation."

Her face froze, and she looked away from him, making him swear under his breath. Without another word she jerked the papers from him and began sorting them, then put them in order by dates. He settled back in his big chair, his face brooding as he watched her enter the figures swiftly and neatly in the ledger, then run the columns through the adding machine twice to make certain they were correct.

When she was finished, she pushed the ledger across the desk. "Check it so you'll be satisfied I didn't make any mistakes."

He did, thoroughly. Finally he closed the ledger and said, "All right."

Her eyes narrowed. "Is that all you have to say? No wonder you've never been married, if you think women don't have the brains to add two and two!"

"I've been married," he said sharply.

The information stunned her, because she'd never heard anyone mention his being married, nor was marriage something she readily associated with John Rafferty. Then hot jealousy seared her at the thought of some other woman living with him, sharing his name and his bed, having the right to touch him. "Who . . . when?" she stammered.

"A long time ago. I'd just turned nineteen, and I had more hormones than sense. God only knows why she married me. It only took her four months to decide ranch life wasn't for her, that she wanted money to spend and a husband who didn't work twenty hours a day."

His voice was flat, his eyes filled with contempt. Michelle felt cold. "Why didn't anyone ever mention it?" she whispered. "I've known you for ten years, but I didn't know you'd been married."

He shrugged. "We got divorced seven years before you moved down here, so it wasn't exactly the hottest news in the county. It didn't last long enough for folks to get to know her, anyway. I worked too much to do any socializing. If she married me thinking a rancher's wife would live in the lap of luxury, she changed her mind in a hurry."

"Where is she now?" Michelle fervently hoped the woman didn't still live in the area.

"I don't know, and I don't care. I heard she married some old rich guy as soon as our divorce was final. It didn't matter to me then, and it doesn't matter now."

It was beyond her how any woman could choose another man, no matter how rich, over John. She would live in a hut and eat rattlesnake meat if it meant staying with him. But she was beginning to understand why he was so contemptuous of the jet-setters, the idle rich, why he'd made so many caustic remarks to her in the past about letting others support her instead of working to support herself. Considering that, it was even more confusing that now he didn't want her doing anything at all, as if he wanted to make her totally dependent on him.

He was watching her from beneath hooded lids, wondering what she was thinking. She'd been shocked to learn he'd been married before. It had been so long ago that he never thought about it, and he wouldn't even have mentioned it if her crack about marriage hadn't reminded him. It had happened in another lifetime, to a nineteen-year-old boy busting his guts to make a go of the rundown little ranch he'd inherited. Sometimes he couldn't even remember her name, and it had been years since he'd been able to remember what she looked like. He wouldn't recognize her if they met face to face.

It was odd, because even though he hadn't seen Michelle during the years of her marriage, he'd never forgotten her face, the way she moved, the way sunlight looked in her hair. He knew every line of her striking, but too angular face, all high cheekbones, stubborn chin and wide, soft mouth. She had put her mouth to his chest and tasted his salty, sweaty skin, her tongue licking at him. She looked so cool and untouchable now in that spotless white dress, but when he made love to her she turned into liquid heat. He thought of the way her legs wrapped around his waist, and he began to harden as desire heated his body. He leaned back in his chair, shifting restlessly.

Michelle had turned back to the stack of papers on his desk, not wanting to pry any further. She didn't want to know any more about his ex-wife, and she especially didn't want him to take the opportunity to ask about her failed marriage. It would be safer to get back to business; she needed to talk to him about selling her beef cattle, anyway.

"I need your advice on something. I wanted to fatten the cattle up for sale this year, but I need operating capital, so I think I should sell them now. Who do I contact, and how is transportation arranged?"

Right at that moment he didn't give a damn about any cattle. She had crossed her legs, and her skirt had slid up a little, drawing his eyes. He wanted to slide it up more, crumple it around her waist and completely bare her legs. His jeans were under considerable strain, and he had to force himself to answer. "Let the cattle fatten; you'll get a lot more money for them. I'll keep the ranch going until then."

She turned her head with a quick, impatient movement, sending her hair swirling, but whatever she had been about to say died when their eyes met and she read his expression. "Let's go upstairs," he murmured.

It was almost frightening to have that intense sexuality focused on her, but she was helpless to resist him. She found herself standing, shivering as he put his hand on her back and ushered her upstairs. Walking beside him made her feel vulnerable; sometimes his size overwhelmed her, and this was one of those times. He was so tall and powerful, his shoulders so broad, that when she lay beneath him in bed he blocked out the light. Only his own control and tenderness protected her.

He locked the bedroom door behind them, then stood behind her and slowly began unzipping her dress. He felt her shivering. "Don't be afraid, baby. Or is it excitement?"

"Yes," she whispered as he slid his hands inside the open dress and around to cup her bare breasts, molding his fingers over her. She could feel her nipples throb against his palms, and with a little whimper she leaned back against him, trying to sink herself into his hardness and warmth. It felt so good when he touched her.

"Both?" he murmured. "Why are you afraid?"

Her eyes were closed, her breath coming in shallow gulps as he rubbed her nipples to hard little points of fire. "The way you make me feel," she gasped, her head rolling on his shoulder.

"You make me feel the same." His voice was slow and guttural as the hot pressure built in him. "Hot, like I'll explode if I don't get inside you. Then you're so soft and tight around me that I know I'm going to explode anyway."

The words made love to her, turning her shivers into shudders. Her legs were liquid, unable to support her; if it hadn't been for John's muscular body behind her, she would have fallen. She whispered his name, the single word vibrant with longing.

His warm breath puffed around her ear as he nuzzled the lobe. "You're so sexy, baby. This dress has been driving me crazy. I wanted to pull up your skirt...like this...." His hands had left her breasts and gone down to her hips, and now her skirt rose along her thighs as he gathered the material in his fists. Then it was at her waist, and his hands were beneath it, his fingers spread over her bare stomach. "I thought about sliding my hands under your panties...like this. Pulling them down...like this."

She moaned as he slipped her panties down her hips and over her buttocks, overcome by a sense of voluptuous helplessness and exposure. Somehow being only partially undressed made her feel even more naked and vulnerable. His long fingers went between her legs, and she quivered like a wild thing as he stroked and probed, slowly building her tension and pleasure to the breaking point.

"You're so sweet and soft," he whispered. "Are you ready for me?"

She tried to answer, but all she could do was gasp. She was on fire, her entire body throbbing, and still he held her against him, his fingers slowly thrusting into her, when he knew she wanted him and was ready for him. He *knew* it. He was too experienced not to know, but he persisted in that sweet torment as he savored the feel of her.

She felt as sexy as he told her she was; her own sensuality was unfolding like a tender flower under his hands and his low, rough voice. Each time he made love to her, she found a little more self-assurance in her own capacity for giving and receiving pleasure. He was strongly, frankly sexual, so experienced that she wanted to slap him every time she thought about it, but she had discovered that she could satisfy him. Sometimes he trembled with hunger when he touched her; this man, whose raw virility gave him sensual power over any woman he wanted, trembled with the need for *her*. She was twenty-eight years old, and only now, in John's hands, was she discovering her power and pleasure as a woman.

Finally she couldn't take any more and whirled away from his hands, her eyes fierce as she stripped off her dress and reached for him, tearing at his clothes. He laughed deeply, but the sound was of excitement rather than humor, and helped her. Naked, already entwined, they fell together to the bed. He took her with a slow, strong thrust, for the first time not having to enter her by careful degrees, and the inferno roared out of control.

Michelle bounced out of bed before he did the next morning, her face glowing. "You don't have to get up," he rumbled in his hoarse, early-morning voice. "Why don't you sleep late?" Actually he liked the thought of her dozing in his bed, rosily naked and exhausted after a night of making love.

She pushed her pale, tousled hair out of her eyes, momentarily riveted by his nudity as he got out of bed. "I'm going with you today," she said, and dashed to beat him to the bathroom.

He joined her in the shower a few minutes later, his black eyes narrowed after her announcement. She waited for him to tell her that she couldn't go, but instead he muttered, "I guess it's okay, if it'll make you happy."

It did. She had decided that John was such an overprotective chauvinist that he would cheerfully keep her wrapped in cotton, so reasoning with him was out of the question. She knew what she could do; she would do it. It was that simple.

Over the next three weeks a deep happiness began forming inside her. She had taken over the paperwork completely, working on it three days out of the week, which gave John more free time at night than he'd ever had before. He gave up checking her work, because he never found an error. On the other days she rode with him, content with his company, and he discovered that he liked having her nearby. There were times when he was so hot, dirty and aggravated that he'd be turning the air blue with savage curses, then he'd look up and catch her smiling at him, and his aggravation would fade away. What did a contrary steer matter when she looked at him that way? She never seemed to mind the dust and heat, or the smells. It wasn't what he'd expected, and sometimes it bothered him. It was as if she were hiding here, burying herself in this self-contained world. The Michelle he'd known before had been a laughing, teasing, social creature, enjoying parties and dancing. This Michelle seldom laughed, though she was so generous with her smiles that it took him a while to notice. One of those smiles made him and all his men a little giddy, but he could remember her sparkling laughter, and he wondered where it had gone.

But it was still so new, having her to himself, that he wasn't anxious to share her with others. They spent the nights tangled together in heated passion, and instead of abating, the hunger only intensified. He spent the days in constant, low-level arousal, and sometimes all he had to do was look at her and he'd be so hard he'd have to find some way of disguising it.

One morning Michelle remained at the house to work in the office; she was alone because Edie had gone grocery shopping. The telephone rang off the hook that morning, interrupting her time and again. She was already irritated with it when it jangled yet again and made her stop what she was doing to answer it. "Rafferty residence."

No one answered, though she could hear slow, deep breathing, as though whoever was on the other end was deliberately controlling his breath. It wasn't a "breather," though; the sound wasn't obscenely exaggerated.

"Hello," she said. "Can you hear me?"

A quiet click sounded in her ear, as if whoever had been calling had put down the receiver with slow, controlled caution, much as he'd been breathing.

He. For some reason she had no doubt it was a man. Common sense said it could be some bored teenager playing a prank, or simply a wrong number, but a sudden chill swept over her.

A sense of menace had filled the silence on the line. For the first time in three weeks she felt isolated and somehow threatened, though there was no tangible reason for it. The chills wouldn't stop running up and down her spine, and suddenly she had to get out of the house, into the hot sunshine. She had to see John, just be able to look at him and hear his deep voice roaring curses, or crooning gently to a horse or a frightened calf. She needed his heat to dispel the coldness of a menace she couldn't define.

Two days later there was another phone call and again, by chance, she answered the phone. "Hello," she said. "Rafferty residence."

Silence.

Her hand began shaking. She strained her ears and heard that quiet, even breathing, then the click as the phone was hung up, and a moment later the dial tone began buzzing in her ear. She felt sick and cold, without knowing why. What was going on? Who was doing this to her?

Chapter 8

Michelle paced the bedroom like a nervous cat, her silky hair swirling around her head as she moved. "I don't feel like going," she blurted. "Why didn't you ask me before you told Addie we'd be there?"

"Because you'd have come up with one excuse after another why you couldn't go, just like you're doing now," he answered calmly. He'd been watching her pace back and forth, her eyes glittering, her usually sinuous movements jerky with agitation. It had been almost a month since he'd moved her to the ranch, and she had yet to stir beyond the boundaries of his property, except to visit her own. He'd given her the keys to the Mercedes and free use of it, but to his knowledge she'd never taken it out. She hadn't been shopping, though he'd made certain she had money. He had received the usual invitations to the neighborhood Saturday night barbecues that had become a county tradition, but she'd always found some excuse not to attend.

He'd wondered fleetingly if she were ashamed of having come down in the world, embarrassed because he didn't measure up financially or in terms of sophistication with the men she'd known before, but he'd dismissed the notion almost before it formed. It wasn't that. He'd come to know her better than that. She came into his arms at night too eagerly, too hungrily, to harbor any feelings that he was socially inferior. A lot of his ideas about her had been wrong. She didn't look down on work, never had. She had simply been sheltered from it her entire life. She was willing to work. Damn it, she insisted on it! He had to watch her to keep her from trying her hand at bulldogging. He was as bad as her father had ever been, willing to do just about anything to keep her happy.

Maybe she was embarrassed because they were living together. This was a rural section, where mores and morality changed slowly. Their arrangement wouldn't so much as raise an eyebrow in Miami or any other large city, but they weren't in a large city. John was too self-assured and arrogant to worry about gossip; he thought of Michelle simply as his woman, with all the fierce possessiveness implied by the term. She was his. He'd held her beneath him and made her his, and the bond was reinforced every time he took her.

Whatever her reason for hiding on the ranch, it was time for it to end. If she were trying to hide their relationship, he wasn't going to let her get away with it any longer. She had to become accustomed to being his woman. He sensed that she was still hiding something of herself from him, carefully preserving a certain distance between them, and it enraged him. It wasn't a physical distance. Sweet Lord, no. She was liquid fire in his arms. The distance was mental; there were times when she was silent and withdrawn, the sparkle gone from her eyes, but whenever he asked her what was wrong she would stonewall, and no amount of probing would induce her to tell him what she'd been thinking.

He was determined to destroy whatever it was that pulled her away from him; he wanted all of her, mind and body. He wanted to hear her laugh, to make her lose her temper as he'd used to do, to hear the haughtiness and petulance in her voice. It was all a part of her, the part she wasn't giving him now, and he wanted it. Damn it, was she tiptoeing around him because she thought she *owed* him?

She hadn't stopped pacing. Now she sat down on the bed and stared at him, her lips set. "I don't want to go."

"I thought you liked Addie." He pulled off his boots and stood to shrug out of his shirt.

"I do," Michelle said.

"Then why don't you want to go to her party? Have you even seen her since you've been back?"

"No, but Dad had just died, and I wasn't in the mood to socialize! Then there was so much work to be done...."

"You don't have that excuse now."

She glared at him. "I decided you were a bully when I was eighteen years old, and nothing you've done over the years has changed my opinion!"

He couldn't stop the grin that spread over his face as he stripped off his jeans. She was something when she got on her high horse. Going over to the bed, he sat beside her and rubbed her back. "Just relax," he soothed. "You know everyone who'll be there, and it's as informal as it always was. You used to have fun at these things, didn't you? They haven't changed."

Michelle let him coax her into lying against his shoulder. She would sound crazy if she told him that she didn't feel safe away from the ranch. He'd want to know why, and what could she tell him? That she'd had two phone calls and the other person wouldn't say anything, just quietly hung up? That happened to people all the time when someone had dialed a wrong number. But she couldn't shake the feeling that something menacing was waiting out there for her if she left the sanctuary of the ranch, where John Rafferty ruled supreme. She sighed, turning her face into his throat. She was overreacting to a simple wrong number; she'd felt safe enough all the time she'd been alone at her house. This was just another little emotional legacy from her marriage.

She gave in. "All right, I'll go. What time does it start?"

"In about two hours." He kissed her slowly, feeling the tension drain out of her, but he could still sense a certain distance in her, as if her mind were on something else, and frustration rose in him. He couldn't pinpoint it, but he knew it was there.

Michelle slipped from his arms, shaking her head as she stood. "You gave me just enough time to get ready, didn't you?"

"We could share a shower," he invited, dropping his last garment at his feet. He stretched, his powerful torso rippling with muscle, and Michelle couldn't take her eyes off him. "I don't mind being late if you don't."

She swallowed. "Thanks, but you go ahead." She was nervous about this party. Even aside from the spooky feeling those phone calls had given her, she wasn't certain how she felt about going. She didn't know how much the ranching crowd knew of her circumstances, but she certainly didn't want anyone pitying her, or making knowing remarks about her position in John's house. On the other hand, she didn't remember anyone as being malicious, and she had always liked Addie Layfield and her husband, Steve. This would be a family oriented group, ranging in age from Frank and Yetta Campbell, in their seventies, to the young children of several families. People would sit around and talk, eat barbecue and drink beer, the children and some of the adults would swim, and the thing would break up of its own accord at about ten o'clock.

John was waiting for her when she came out of the bathroom after showering and dressing. She had opted for cool and comfortable, sleeking her wet hair straight back and twisting it into a knot, which she'd pinned at her nape, and she wore a minimum of makeup. She had on an oversize white cotton T-shirt, with the tail tied in a knot on one hip, and loose white cotton drawstring pants. Her sandals consisted of soles and two straps each. On someone else the same ensemble might have looked sloppy, but on Michelle it looked chic. He decided she could wear a feed sack and make it look good.

"Don't forget your swimsuit," he said, remembering that she had always gone swimming at these parties. She'd loved the water.

Michelle looked away, pretending to check her purse for something. "I'm not swimming tonight."

"Why not?"

"I just don't feel like it."

Her voice had that flat, expressionless sound he'd come to hate, the same tone she used whenever he tried to probe into the reason she sometimes became so quiet and distant. He looked at her sharply, and his brows drew together. He couldn't remember Michelle ever "not feeling" like swimming. Her father had put in a pool for her the first year they'd been in Florida, and she had often spent the entire day lolling in the water. After she'd married, the pool had gone unused and had finally been emptied. He didn't think it had ever been filled again, and now it was badly in need of repairs before it would be usable.

But she'd been with him almost a month, and he didn't think she'd been in his pool even once. He glanced out at the balcony; he could just see a corner of the pool, blue and glittering in the late afternoon sun. He didn't have much time for swimming, but he'd insisted, eight years ago, on having the big pool and its luxurious landscaping. For her. Damn it, this whole place was for her: the big house, the comforts, that pool, even the damn Mercedes. He'd built it for her, not admitting it to himself then because he couldn't. Why wasn't she using the pool?

Michelle could feel his sharpened gaze on her as they left the room, but he didn't say anything and, relieved, she realized he was going to let it go. Maybe he just accepted that she didn't feel like swimming. If he only knew how much she wanted to swim, how she'd longed for the feel of cool water on her overheated skin, but she just couldn't bring herself to put on a bathing suit, even in the privacy of his house.

She knew that the little white scars were hardly visible now, but she still shrank from the possibility that someone might notice them. She still felt that they were glaringly obvious, even though the mirror told her differently. It had become such a habit to hide them that she couldn't stop. She didn't dress or undress in front of John if she could help it, and if she couldn't, she always remained facing him, so he wouldn't see her back. It was such a reversal of modesty that he hadn't even noticed her reluctance to be nude in front of him. At night, in bed, it didn't matter. If the lights were on, they were dim, and John had other things on his mind. Still she insisted on wearing a nightgown to bed. It might be off most of the night, but it would be on when she got out of bed in the mornings. Everything in her shrank from having to explain those scars.

The party was just as she had expected, with a lot of food, a lot of talk, a lot of laughter. Addie had once been one of Michelle's best friends, and she was still the warm, talkative person she'd been before. She'd put on a little weight, courtesy of two children, but her pretty face still glowed with good humor. Steve, her husband, sometimes managed to put his own two cents into a conversation by the simple means of putting his hand over her mouth. Addie laughed more than anyone whenever he resorted to that tactic.

"It's an old joke between us," she told Michelle as they put together tacos for the children. "When we were dating, he'd do that so he could kiss me. Holy cow, you look good! Something must be agreeing with you, and I'd say that 'something' is about six-foot-three of pure hunk. God, I used to swoon whenever he spoke to me! Remember? You'd sniff and say he

didn't do anything for you. Liar, liar, pants on fire.''
Addie chanted the childish verse, her eyes sparkling
with mirth, and Michelle couldn't help laughing with
her.

On the other side of the pool, John's head swiveled
at the sound, and he froze, stunned by the way her
face lit as she joked with Addie. He felt the hardening
in his loins and swore silently to himself, jerking his
attention back to the talk of cattle and shifting his
position to make his arousal less obvious. Why didn't
she laugh like that more often?

Despite Michelle's reservations, she enjoyed the
party. She'd missed the relaxed gatherings, so different from the sophisticated dinner parties, yacht parties, divorce parties, fund-raising dinners, et cetera,
that had made up the social life John thought she'd
enjoyed so much, but had only tolerated. She liked the
shrieks of the children as they cannonballed into the
pool, splashing any unwary adult in the vicinity, and
she liked it that no one got angry over being wet.
Probably it felt good in the sweltering heat, which had
abated only a little.

True to most of the parties she'd attended, the men
tended to group together and the women did the same,
with the men talking cattle and weather, and the
women talking about people. But the groups were
fluid, flowing together and intermingling, and by the
time the children had worn down, all the adults were
sitting together. John had touched her arm briefly
when he sat down beside her, a small, possessive gesture that made her tingle. She tried not to stare at him
like an infatuated idiot, but she felt as if everyone
there could tell how warm she was getting. Her cheeks

flushed, and she darted a glance at him to find him watching her with blatant need.

"Let's go home," he said in a low voice.

"So soon?" Addie protested, but at that moment they all heard the distant rumble of thunder.

As ranchers, they all searched the night sky for signs of a storm that would break the heat, if only for a little while, and fill the slow-moving rivers and streams. Out to the west, over the Gulf, lightning shimmered in a bank of black clouds.

Frank Campbell said, "We sure could use a good rain. Haven't had one in about a month now."

It had stormed the day John had come over to her ranch for the first time, Michelle remembered, and again the night they'd driven back from Tampa...the first time he'd made love to her. His eyes glittered, and she knew he was thinking the same thing.

Wind suddenly kicked up from the west, bringing with it the cool smell of rain and salt, the excitement of a storm. Everyone began gathering up children and food, cleaning up the patio before the rain hit. Soon people were calling out goodbyes and piling into pickup trucks and cars.

"Glad you went?" John asked as he turned onto the highway.

Michelle was watching the lacy patterns the lightning made as it forked across the sky. "Yes, I had fun." She moved closer against him, seeking his warmth.

He held the truck steady against the gusts of wind buffeting it, feeling her breast brush his arm every time he moved. He inhaled sharply at his inevitable response.

"What's wrong?" she asked sleepily.

For answer he took her hand and pressed it to the straining fabric of his jeans. She made a soft sound, and her slender fingers outlined the hard ridge beneath the fabric as her body automatically curled toward him. He felt his jeans open; then her hand slid inside the parted fabric and closed over him, her palm soft and warm. He groaned aloud, his body jerking as he tried to keep his attention on the road. It was the sweetest torture he could imagine, and he ground his teeth as her hand moved further down to gently cup him for a moment before returning to stroke him to the edge of madness.

He wanted her, and he wanted her now. Jerking the steering wheel, he pulled the truck onto the side of the road just as fat raindrops began splattering the windshield. "Why are we stopping?" Michelle murmured.

He killed the lights and reached for her, muttering a graphic explanation.

"John! We're on the highway! Anyone could pass by and see us!"

"It's dark and raining," he said roughly, untying the drawstring at her waist and pulling her pants down. "No one can see in."

She'd been enjoying teasing him, exciting him, exciting herself with the feel of his hardness in her hand, but she'd thought he would wait until they got home. She should have known better. He didn't care if they were in a bedroom or not; his appetites were strong and immediate. She went weak under the onslaught of his mouth and hands, no longer caring about anything else. The rain was a thunderous din, streaming over the windows of the truck as if they were sitting under a waterfall. She could barely hear the rawly sexual things he was saying to her as he slid to the middle of the seat and lifted her over him. She cried out at his penetration, her body arching in his hands, and the world spun away in a whirlwind of sensations.

Later, after the rain had let up, she was limp in his arms as he carried her inside the house. Her hands slid around his neck as he bent to place her gently on the bed, and obeying that light pressure he stretched out on the bed with her. She was exhausted, sated, her body still throbbing with the remnants of pleasure. He kissed her deeply, rubbing his hand over her breasts and stomach. "Do you want me to undress you?" he murmured.

She nuzzled his throat. "No, I'll do it . . . in a minute. I don't feel like moving right now."

His big hand paused on her stomach, then slipped lower. "We didn't use anything."

"It's okay," she assured him softly. The timing was wrong. She had just finished her cycle, which was one reason he'd exploded out of control.

He rubbed his lips over hers in warm, quick kisses. "I'm sorry, baby. I was so damned ready for you, I thought I was going to go off like a teenager."

"It's okay," she said again. She loved him so much she trembled with it. Sometimes it was all she could do to keep from telling him, from crying the words aloud, but she was terrified that if she did he'd start putting distance between them, wary of too many entanglements. It had to end sometime, but she wanted it to last every possible second.

Nothing terrible had happened to her because she'd gone to the party; in fact, the trip home had been wonderful. For days afterward, she shivered with delight whenever she thought about it. There hadn't been any other out of the ordinary phone calls, and gradually she relaxed, convinced that there had been nothing to them. She was still far more content remaining on the ranch than she was either socializing or shopping, but at John's urging she began using the Mercedes to run small errands and occasionally visit her friends on those days when she wasn't riding with him or working on the books. She drove over to her house several times to check on things, but the silence depressed her. John had had the electricity turned back on, though he hadn't mentioned it to her, but she didn't say anything about moving back in. She couldn't leave him, not now; she was so helplessly, hopelessly in love with him that she knew she'd stay with him until he told her to leave.

One Monday afternoon she'd been on an errand for John, and on the return trip she detoured by her house to check things again. She walked through the huge rooms, making certain no pipes had sprung a leak or anything else needed repair. It was odd; she hadn't been away that long, but the house felt less and less like her home. It was hard to remember how it had been before John Rafferty had come storming into her life again; his presence was so intense it blocked out lesser details. Her troubled dreams had almost disappeared, and even when she had one, she would wake to find him beside her in the night, strong and warm. It was becoming easier to trust, to accept that she wasn't alone to face whatever happened.

It was growing late, and the shadows lengthened in the house; she carefully locked the door behind her and walked out to the car. Abruptly she shivered, as if something cold had touched her. She looked around, but everything was normal. Birds sang in the trees; insects hummed. But for a moment she'd felt it again, that sense of menace. It was odd.

Logic told her there was nothing to it, but when she was in the car she locked the doors. She laughed a little at herself. First a couple of phone calls had seemed spooky, and now she was "feeling" things in the air.

Because there was so little traffic on the secondary roads between her ranch and John's, she didn't use the rearview mirrors very much. The car was on her rear bumper before she noticed it, and even then she got only a glimpse before it swung to the left to pass. The road was narrow, and she edged to the right to give the other car more room. It pulled even with her, and she gave it a cursory glance just as it suddenly swerved toward her.

"Watch it!" she yelled, jerking the steering wheel to the right, but there was a loud grinding sound as metal rubbed against metal. The Mercedes, smaller than the other car, was pushed violently to the right. Michelle slammed on the brakes as she felt the two right wheels catch in the sandy soil of the shoulder, pulling the car even harder to that side.

She wrestled with the steering wheel, too scared even to swear at the other driver. The other car shot past, and somehow she managed to jerk the Mercedes back onto the road. Shaking, she braked to a stop and leaned her head on the steering wheel, then sat upright as she heard tires squealing. The other car had gone down the road, but now had made a violent U-turn and was coming back. She only hoped whoever it was had insurance.

The car was a big, blue full-size Chevrolet. She could tell that a man was driving, because the silhouette was so large. It was only a silhouette, because he had something black pulled over his head, like a ski mask.

The coldness was back. She acted instinctively, jamming her foot onto the gas pedal, and the sporty little Mercedes leaped forward. The Chevrolet swerved toward her again, and she swung wildly to the side. She almost missed it…almost. The Chevrolet clipped her rear bumper, and the smaller, lighter car spun in a nauseating circle before sliding off the road, across the wide sandy shoulder, and scraping against an enormous pine before it bogged down in the soft dirt and weeds.

She heard herself screaming, but the hard jolt that stopped the car stopped her screams, too. Dazed, her head lolled against the broken side window for a moment before terror drove the fogginess away. She groped for the handle, but couldn't budge the door. The pine tree blocked it. She tried to scramble across the seat to the other door, and only then realized she was still buckled into her seat. Fumbling, looking around wildly for the Chevrolet, she released the buckle and threw herself to the other side of the car. She pushed the door open and tumbled out in the same motion, her breath wheezing in and out of her lungs.

Numbly she crouched by the fender and tried to listen, but she could hear nothing over her tortuous breathing and the thunder of her heart. Old habits took over, and she used a trick she'd often used before to calm herself after one of Roger's insane rages, taking a deep breath and holding it. The maneuver slowed her heartbeat almost immediately, and the roar faded out of her ears.

She couldn't hear anything. Oh, God, had he stopped? Cautiously she peered over the car, but she couldn't see the blue Chevrolet.

Slowly she realized it had gone. He hadn't stopped. She stumbled to the road and looked in both directions, but the road was empty.

She couldn't believe it had happened. He had deliberately run her off the road, not once, but twice. If the small Mercedes had hit one of the huge pines that thickly lined the road head-on, she could easily have been killed. Whoever the man was, he must have figured the heavier Chevrolet could muscle her off the road without any great risk to himself.

He'd tried to kill her.

It was five minutes before another car came down the road; it was blue, and for a horrible moment she panicked, thinking the Chevrolet was returning, but as it came closer she could tell this car was much older and wasn't even a Chevrolet. She stumbled to the middle of the road, waving her arms to flag it down.

All she could think of was John. She wanted John. She wanted him to hold her close and shut the terror away with his strength and possessiveness. Her voice shook as she leaned in the window and told the young boy, "Please—call John Rafferty. Tell him I've been . . . I've had an accident. Tell him I'm all right."

"Sure, lady," the boy said. "What's your name?"

"Michelle," she said. "My name's Michelle."

The boy looked at the car lodged against the pine. "You need a wrecker, too. Are you sure you're all right?"

"Yes, I'm not hurt. Just hurry, please."

"Sure thing."

Either John called the sheriff's department or the boy had, because John and a county sheriff's car arrived from opposite directions almost simultaneously. It hadn't been much more than ten minutes since the boy had stopped, but in that short length of time it had grown considerably darker. John threw his door open as the truck ground to a stop and was out of the vehicle before it had settled back on its wheels, striding toward her. She couldn't move toward him; she was shaking too violently. Beneath his mustache his lips were a thin, grim line.

He walked all the way around her, checking her from head to foot. Only when he didn't see any blood on her did he haul her against his chest, his arms so tight they almost crushed her. He buried his hand in her hair and bent his head down until his jaw rested on her temple. "Are you really all right?" he muttered hoarsely.

Her arms locked around his waist in a death grip. "I was wearing my seat belt," she whispered. A single tear slid unnoticed down her cheek.

"God, when I got that phone call—" He broke off, because there was no way he could describe the stark terror he'd felt despite the kid's assurance that she was okay. He'd had to see her for himself, hold her, before he could really let himself believe she wasn't harmed. If he'd seen blood on her, he would have gone berserk. Only now was his heartbeat settling down, and he looked over her head at the car.

The deputy approached them, clipboard in hand. "Can you answer a few questions, ma'am?"

John's arms dropped from around her, but he remained right beside her as she answered the usual questions about name, age and driver's license number. When the deputy asked her how it had happened, she began shaking again.

"A...a car ran me off the road," she stammered. "A blue Chevrolet."

The deputy looked up, his eyes abruptly interested as a routine accident investigation became something more. "Ran you off the road? How?"

"He sideswiped me." Fiercely she clenched her fingers together in an effort to still their trembling. "He pushed me off the road."

"He didn't just come too close, and you panicked and ran off the road?" John asked, his brows drawing together.

"No! He pushed me off the road. I slammed on my brakes and he went on past, then turned around and came back."

"He came back? Did you get his name?" The deputy made a notation on his pad. Leaving the scene of an accident was a crime.

"No, he didn't stop. He...he tried to ram me. He hit my bumper, and I spun off the road, then into that pine tree."

John jerked his head at the deputy and they walked over to the car, bending down to inspect the damage. They talked together in low voices; Michelle couldn't make out what they were saying, but she didn't move closer. She stood by the road, listening to the peaceful sounds of the deepening Florida twilight. It was all so out of place. How could the crickets be chirping so happily when someone had just tried to commit murder? She felt dazed, as if none of this were real. But the damaged car was real. The blue Chevrolet had been real, as had the man wearing the black ski mask.

The two men walked back toward her. John looked at her sharply; her face was deathly white, even in the growing gloom, and she was shaking. She looked terrified. The Mercedes *was* an expensive car; did she expect him to tear a strip off her hide because she'd wrecked it? She'd never had to worry about things like that before, never had to be accountable for anything. If she'd banged a fender, it hadn't been important; her father had simply had the car repaired, or bought her a new one. Hell, he wasn't happy that she'd wrecked the damn car, but he wasn't a fanatic about cars, no matter how much they cost. It would have been different if she'd ruined a good horse. He was just thankful she wasn't hurt.

"It's all right," he said, trying to soothe her as he took her arm and walked her to the truck. "I have insurance on it. You're okay, and that's what matters. Just calm down. I'll take you home as soon as the deputy's finished with his report and the wrecker gets here."

Frantically she clutched his arm. "But what about—"

He kissed her and rubbed her shoulder. "I said it's all right, baby. I'm not mad. You don't have to make excuses."

Frozen, Michelle sat in the truck and watched as he walked back to the deputy. He didn't believe her; neither of them believed her. It was just like before, when no one would believe handsome, charming Roger Beckman was capable of hitting his wife, because it was obvious he adored her. It was just too unbelievable. Even her father had thought she was exaggerating.

She was so cold, even though the temperature was still in the nineties. She had begun to trust, to accept that John stood behind her, as unmoving as a block of granite, his strength available whenever she needed him. For the first time she hadn't felt alone. He'd been there, ready to shoulder her burdens. But suddenly it was just like before, and she was cold and alone again. Her father had given her everything materially, but had been too weak to face an ugly truth. Roger had showered her with gifts, pampering her extravagantly to make up for the bruises and terror. John had given her a place to live, food to eat, mind-shattering physical pleasure... but now he, too, was turning away from a horribly real threat. It was too much effort to believe such a tale. Why would anyone try to kill her?

She didn't know, but someone had. The phone calls... the phone calls were somehow connected. They'd given her the same feeling she'd had just before she got in the car, the same sense of menace. God, had he been watching her at her house? Had he been waiting for her? He could be anywhere. He knew her, but she didn't know him, and she was alone again. She'd always been alone, but she hadn't known it. For a while she'd trusted, hoped, and the contrast with that warm feeling of security made cold reality just that much more piercing.

The wrecker arrived with its yellow lights flashing and backed up to the Mercedes. Michelle watched with detached interest as the car was hauled away from the pine. She didn't even wince at the amount of damage that had been done to the left side. John thought she'd made up a wild tale to keep from having to accept blame for wrecking the car. He didn't believe her. The deputy didn't believe her. There should be blue paint on the car, but evidently the scrapes left by the big pine had obscured it. Maybe dirt covered it. Maybe it was too dark for them to see. For whatever reason, they didn't believe her.

She was utterly silent as John drove home. Edie came to the door, watching anxiously, then hurried forward as Michelle slid out of the truck.

"Are you all right? John left here like a bat out of hell, didn't stop to tell us anything except you'd had an accident."

"I'm fine," Michelle murmured. "I just need a bath. I'm freezing."

Frowning, John touched her arm. It was icy, despite the heat. She wasn't hurt, but she'd had a shock.

"Make some coffee," he instructed Edie as he turned Michelle toward the stairs. "I'll give her a bath."

Slowly Michelle pulled away from him. Her face was calm. "No, I'll do it. I'm all right. Just give me a few minutes by myself."

After a hot but brief shower, she went downstairs and drank coffee, and even managed to eat a few bites of the meal Edie had put back when John tore out of the house.

In bed that night, for the first time she couldn't respond to him. He needed her almost desperately, to reassure himself once again that she was truly all right. He needed to strengthen the bond between them, to draw her even closer with ties as old as time. But though he was gentle and stroked her for a long time, she remained tense under his hands. She was still too quiet, somehow distant from him.

Finally he just held her, stroking her hair until she slept and her soft body relaxed against him. But he lay awake for hours, his body burning, his eyes open. God, how close he'd come to losing her!

Chapter 9

John listened impatiently, his hard, dark face angry, his black eyes narrowed. Finally he said, "It hasn't been three months since I straightened all that out. How the hell did you manage to get everything in a mess this fast?"

Michelle looked up from the figures she was posting in, curious to learn the identity of his caller. He hadn't said much more than hello before he'd begun getting angry. Finally he said, "All right. I'll be down tomorrow. And if you're out partying when I get there, the way you were last time, I'll turn around and come home. I don't have time to cool my heels while you're playing." He hung up the phone and muttered a graphic expletive.

"Who was it?" Michelle asked.

"Mother." A wealth of irritation was in the single word.

She was stunned. "*Your* mother?"

He looked at her for a moment; then his mustache twitched a little as he almost smiled. "You don't have to sound so shocked. I got here by the normal method."

"But you've never mentioned ... I guess I assumed she was dead, like your father."

"She cut out a long time ago. Ranching wasn't good enough for her; she liked the bright lights of Miami and the money of Palm Beach, so she walked out one fine day and never came back."

"How old were you?"

"Six or seven, something like that. Funny, I don't remember being too upset when she left, or missing her very much. Mostly I remember how she used to complain because the house was small and old, and because there was never much money. I was with Dad every minute I wasn't in school, but I was never close to Mother."

She felt as she had when she'd discovered he had been married. He kept throwing out little tidbits about himself, then dismissing these vital points of his life as if they hadn't affected him much at all. Maybe they hadn't. John was a hard man, made so by a lifetime of backbreaking work and the combination of arrogance and steely determination in his personality. But how could a child not be affected when his mother walked away? How could a young man, little more than a boy, not be affected when his new wife walked out rather than work by his side? To this day John would do anything to help someone who was *trying*, but he wouldn't lift a finger to aid anyone who sat around waiting for help. All his employees were loyal to him down to their last drop of blood. If they hadn't been, they wouldn't still be on his ranch.

"When you went to Miami before, it was to see your mother?"

"Yeah. She makes a mess of her finances at least twice a year and expects me to drop everything, fly down there and straighten it out."

"Which you do."

He shrugged. "We may not be close, but she's still my mother."

"Call me this time," she said distinctly, giving him a hard look that underlined her words.

He grunted, looking irritated, then gave her a wink as he turned to call the airlines. Michelle listened as he booked a flight to Miami for the next morning. Then he glanced at her and said "Wait a minute" into the receiver before putting his hand over the mouthpiece. "Want to come with me?" he asked her.

Panic flared in her eyes before she controlled it and shook her head. "No thanks. I need to catch up on the paperwork."

It was a flimsy excuse, as the accumulated work wouldn't take more than a day, but though John gave her a long, level look, he didn't argue with her. Instead he moved his fingers from the mouthpiece and said, "Just one. That's right. No, not round trip. I don't know what day I'll be coming back. Yeah, thanks."

He scribbled his flight number and time on a notepad as he took the phone from his ear and hung up. Since the accident, Michelle hadn't left the ranch at all, for any reason. He'd picked up the newly repaired Mercedes three days ago, but it hadn't been moved from the garage since. Accidents sometimes made people nervous about driving again, but he sensed that something more was bothering her.

She'd begun totalling the figures she had posted in the ledger. His eyes drifted over her, drinking in her serious, absorbed expression and the way she chewed her bottom lip when she was working. She'd taken over his office so completely that he sometimes had to ask *her* questions about what was going on. He wasn't certain he liked having part of the ranch out of his direct control, but he was damn certain he liked the extra time he had at night.

That thought made him realize he'd be spending the next few nights alone, and he scowled. Once he would have found female companionship in Miami, but now he was distinctly uninterested in any other woman. He wanted Michelle and no one else. No other woman had ever fit in his arms as well as she did, or given him the pleasure she gave just by being there. He liked to tease her until she lost her temper and lashed back at him, just for the joy of watching her get snooty. An even greater joy was taking her to bed and loving her out of her snooty moods. Thanks to his mother, it was a joy he'd have to do without for a few days. He didn't like it worth a damn.

Suddenly he realized it wasn't just the sex. He didn't want to leave her, because she was upset about something. He wanted to hold her and make everything right for her, but she wouldn't tell him about it. He felt uneasy. She insisted nothing was wrong, but he knew better. He just didn't know what it was. A couple of times he'd caught her staring out the window with an expression that was almost . . . terrified. He had to be wrong, because she had no reason to be scared. And of what?

It had all started with the accident. He'd been trying to reassure her that he wasn't angry about the car, but instead she'd drawn away from him as if he'd slapped her, and he couldn't bridge the distance between them. For just an instant she'd looked shocked, even hurt, then she'd withdrawn in some subtle way he couldn't describe, but felt. The withdrawal wasn't physical; except for the night of the accident, she was as sweet and wild in his arms as she'd ever been. But he wanted all of her, mind and body, and the accident had only made his wanting more intense by taunting him with the knowledge of how quickly she could be taken away.

He reached out and touched his fingertips to her cheekbone, needing to touch her even in so small a way. Her eyes cut up to him with a flash of green, their gazes catching, locking. Without a word she closed the ledger and stood. She didn't look back as she walked out of the room with the fluid grace he'd always admired and sometimes hated because he couldn't have the body that produced it. But now he could, and as he followed her from the room he was already unbuttoning his shirt. His booted feet were deliberately placed on the stairs, his attention on the bedroom at the top and the woman inside it.

Sometimes, when the days were hot and slow and the sun was a disc of blinding white, Michelle would feel that it had all been a vivid nightmare and hadn't really happened at all. The phone calls had meant nothing. The danger she'd sensed was merely the product of an overactive imagination. The man in the ski mask hadn't tried to kill her. The accident hadn't been a murder attempt disguised to look like an accident. None of that had happened at all. It was only a dream, while reality was Edie humming as she did housework, the stamping and snorting of the horses, the placid cattle grazing in the pastures, John's daily phone calls from Miami that charted his impatience to be back home.

But it hadn't been a dream. John didn't believe her, but his nearness had nevertheless kept the terror at bay and given her a small pocket of safety. She felt secure here on the ranch, ringed by the wall of his authority, surrounded by his people. Without him beside her in the night, her feeling of safety weakened. She was sleeping badly, and during the days she pushed herself as relentlessly as she had when she'd been working her own ranch alone, trying to exhaust her body so she could sleep.

Nev Luther had received his instructions, as usual, but again he was faced with the dilemma of how to carry them out. If Michelle wanted to do something, how was he supposed to stop her? Call the boss in Miami and tattle? Nev didn't doubt for a minute the boss would spit nails and strip hide if he saw Michelle doing the work she was doing, but she didn't *ask* if she could do it, she simply did it. Not much he could do about that. Besides, she seemed to need the work to occupy her mind. She was quieter than usual, probably missing the boss. The thought made Nev smile. He approved of the current arrangement, and would approve even more if it turned out to be permanent.

After four days of doing as much as she could, Michelle was finally exhausted enough that she thought she could sleep, but she put off going to bed. If she were wrong, she'd spend more hours lying tense and sleepless, or shaking in the aftermath of a dream. She forced herself to stay awake and catch up on the paperwork, the endless stream of orders and invoices that chronicled the prosperity of the ranch. It could have waited, but she wanted everything to be in order when John came home. The thought brought a smile to her strained face; he'd be home tomorrow. His afternoon call had done more to ease her mind than anything. Just one more night to get through without him, then he'd be beside her again in the darkness.

She finished at ten, then climbed the stairs and changed into one of the light cotton shifts she slept in. The night was hot and muggy, too hot for her to tolerate even a sheet over her, but she was tired enough that the heat didn't keep her awake. She turned on her side, almost groaning aloud as her muscles relaxed, and was instantly asleep.

It was almost two in the morning when John silently let himself into the house. He'd planned to take an 8:00 a.m. flight, but after talking to Michelle he'd paced restlessly, impatient with the hours between them. He had to hold her close, feel her slender, too fragile body in his arms before he could be certain she was all right. The worry was even more maddening because he didn't know its cause.

Finally he couldn't stand it. He'd called the airport and gotten a seat on the last flight out that night, then thrown his few clothes into his bag and kissed his mother's forehead. "Take it easy on that damned checkbook," he'd growled, looking down at the elegant, shallow and still pretty woman who had given birth to him.

The black eyes he'd inherited looked back at him, and one corner of her crimson lips lifted in the same one-sided smile that often quirked his mouth. "You haven't told me anything, but I've heard rumors even down here," she'd said smoothly. "Is it true you've got Langley Cabot's daughter living with you? Really, John, he lost everything he owned."

He'd been too intent on getting back to Michelle to feel more than a spark of anger. "Not everything."

"Then it's true? She's living with you?"

"Yes."

She had given him a long, steady look. Since he'd been nineteen he'd had a lot of women, but none of them had lived with him, even briefly, and despite the distance between them, or perhaps because of it, she knew her son well. No one took advantage of him. If Michelle Cabot was in his house, it was because he wanted her there, not due to any seductive maneuvers on her part.

As John climbed the stairs in the dark, silent house, his heart began the slow, heavy rhythm of anticipation. He wouldn't wake her, but he couldn't wait to lie beside her again, just to feel the soft warmth of her body and smell the sweetness of her skin. He was tired; he could use a few hours' sleep. But in the morning... Her skin would be rosy from sleep, and she'd stretch drowsily with that feline grace of hers. He would take her then.

Noiselessly he entered the bedroom, shutting the door behind him. She was small and still in the bed, not stirring at his presence. He set his bag down and went into the bathroom. When he came out a few minutes later he left the bathroom light on so he could see while he undressed.

He looked at the bed again, and every muscle in his body tightened. Sweat beaded on his forehead. He couldn't have torn his eyes away even if a tornado had hit the house at that moment.

She was lying half on her stomach, with all the covers shoved down to the foot of the bed. Her right leg was stretched out straight, her left one drawn up toward the middle of the mattress. She was wearing one of those flimsy cotton shifts she liked, and during the night it had worked its way up to her buttocks. She was exposed to him. His burning gaze slowly, agonizingly moved over the bare curves of her buttocks from beneath the thin cotton garment, to the soft, silky female cleft and folds he loved to touch.

He shuddered convulsively, grinding his teeth to hold back the deep, primal sound rumbling in his chest. He'd gotten so hard, so fast, that his entire body ached and throbbed. She was sound asleep, her breath coming in a deep, slow rhythm. His own breath was billowing in and out of his lungs; sweat was pouring out of him, his muscles shaking like a stallion scenting a mare ready for mounting. Without taking his eyes from her he began unbuttoning his shirt. He had to have her; he couldn't wait. She was moist and vulnerable, warm and female, and...his. He was coming apart just looking at her, his control shredded, his loins surging wildly.

He left his clothes on the bedroom floor and bent over her, forcing his hands to gentleness as he turned her onto her back. She made a small sound that wasn't quite a sigh and adjusted her position, but didn't awaken. His need was so urgent that he didn't take the time to wake her; he pulled the shift to her waist, spread her thighs and positioned himself between them. With his last remnant of control he eased into her, a low, rough groan bursting from his throat as her hot, moist flesh tightly sheathed him.

She whimpered a little, her body arching in his hands, and her arms lifted to twine around his neck. "I love you," she moaned, still more asleep than awake. Her words went through him like lightning, his body jerking in response. Oh God, he didn't even know if she said it to him or to some dream, but everything in him shattered. He wanted to hear the words again, and he wanted her awake, her eyes looking into his when she said them, so he'd know who was in her mind. Desperately he sank deeper into her, trying to absorb her body into his so irrevocably that nothing could separate them.

"Michelle," he whispered in taut agony, burying his open mouth against her warm throat.

Michelle lifted, arching toward him again as her mind swam upward out of a sleep so deep it had bordered on unconsciousness. But even asleep she had known his touch, her body reacting immediately to him, opening for him, welcoming him. She didn't question his presence; he was there, and that was all that mattered. A great burst of love so intense that she almost cried out reduced everything else to insignificance. She was on fire, her senses reeling, her flesh shivering under the slamming thrusts of his loins. She felt him deep inside her, touching her, and she screamed into his mouth like a wild creature as sharp ecstasy detonated her nerves. He locked her to him with iron-muscled thighs and arms, holding her as she strained madly beneath him, and the feel of her soft internal shudders milking him sent him blasting into his own hot, sweet insanity.

He couldn't let her go. Even when it was over, he couldn't let her go. He began thrusting again, needing even more of her to satisfy the hunger that went so deep he didn't think it would ever be satisfied.

She was crying a little, her luminous green eyes wet as she clung to him. She said his name in a raw, shaking voice. He hadn't let her slide down to a calm plateau but kept her body tense with desire. He was slow and tender now, gentling her into ecstasy instead of hurling her into it, but the culmination was no less shattering.

It was almost dawn before she curled up in his arms, both of them exhausted. Just before she went to sleep she said in mild surprise, "You came home early."

His arms tightened around her. "I couldn't stand another night away from you." It was the bald, frightening truth. He would have made it back even if he'd had to walk.

No one bothered them the next morning, and they slept until long after the sun began pouring brightly into the room. Nev Luther, seeing John's truck parked in its normal location, came to the house to ask him a question, but Edie dared the foreman to disturb them with such a fierce expression on her face that he decided the question wasn't important after all.

John woke shortly after one, disturbed by the heat of the sunlight streaming directly onto the bed. His temples and mustache were already damp with sweat, and he badly needed a cool shower to drive away the sluggishness of heat and exhaustion. He left the bed quietly, taking care not to wake Michelle, though a purely male smile touched his hard lips as he saw her shift lying in the middle of the floor. He didn't even remember pulling it off her, much less throwing it. Nothing had mattered but loving her.

He stood under the shower, feeling utterly sated but somehow uneasy. He kept remembering the sound of her voice when she said "I love you" and it was driving him crazy. Had she been dreaming, or had she known it was him? She'd never said it before, and she hadn't said it again. The uncertainty knifed at him. It had felt so right, but then, they had always fitted together in bed so perfectly that his memories of other women were destroyed. Out of bed... There was always that small distance he couldn't bridge, that part of herself that she wouldn't let him know. Did she love someone else? Was it one of her old crowd? A tanned, sophisticated jet-setter who was out of her reach now that she didn't have money? The thought tormented him, because he knew it was possible to love someone even when they were far away and years passed between meetings. He knew, because he'd loved Michelle that way.

His face was drawn as he cut the water off with a savage movement. *Love.* God, he'd loved her for years, and lied to himself about it by burying it under hostility, then labeling it as lust, want, need, anything to keep from admitting he was as vulnerable as a naked baby when it came to her. He was hard as nails, a sexual outlaw who casually used and left women, but he'd only prowled from woman to woman so restlessly because none of them had been able to satisfy his hunger. None of them had been the one woman he wanted, the one woman he loved. Now he had her physically, but not mentally, not emotionally, and he was scared spitless. His hands were trembling as he rubbed a towel over his body. Somehow he had to make her love him. He'd use any means necessary to keep her with him, loving her and taking care of her until no one existed in her mind except him, and every part of her became his to cherish.

Would she run if he told her he loved her? If he said the words, would she be uncomfortable around him? He remembered how he'd felt whenever some woman had tried to cling to him, whimpering that she loved him, begging him to stay. He'd felt embarrassment, impatience, pity. Pity! He couldn't take it if Michelle pitied him.

He'd never felt uncertain before. He was arrogant, impatient, determined, and he was used to men jumping when he barked out an order. It was unsettling to discover that he couldn't control either his emotions or Michelle's. He'd read before that love made strong men weak, but he hadn't understood it until now. Weak? Hell, he was terrified!

Naked, he returned to the bedroom and pulled on underwear and jeans. She was a magnet, drawing his eyes to her time and again. Lord, she was something to look at, with that pale gold hair gleaming in the bright sunlight, her bare flesh glowing. She lay on her stomach with her arms under the pillow, giving him a view of her supple back, firmly rounded buttocks and long, sleek legs. He admired her graceful lines and feminine curves, the need growing in him to touch her. Was she going to sleep all day?

He crossed to the bed and sat down on the side, stroking his hand over her bare shoulder. "Wake up, lazybones. It's almost two o'clock."

She yawned, snuggling deeper into the pillow. "So?" Her mouth curved into a smile as she refused to open her eyes.

He chuckled. "So get up. I can't even get dressed when you're lying here like this. My attention keeps wander—'' He broke off, frowning at the small white scar marring the satiny shoulder under his fingers. She was lying naked under the bright rays of the afternoon sun, or he might not have noticed. Then he saw another one, and he touched it, too. His gaze moved, finding more of them marring the perfection of her skin. They were all down her back, even on her bottom and the backs of her upper thighs. His fingers touched all of them, moving slowly from scar to scar. She was rigid under his hands, not moving or looking at him, not even breathing.

Stunned, he tried to think of what could have made those small, crescent-shaped marks. Accidental cuts, by broken glass for instance, wouldn't all have been the same size and shape. The cuts hadn't been deep; the scarring was too faint, with no raised ridges. That was why he hadn't felt them, though he'd touched every inch of her body. But if they weren't accidental, that meant they had to be deliberate.

His indrawn breath hissed roughly through his teeth. He swore, his voice so quiet and controlled that the explicitly obscene words shattered the air more effectively than if he'd roared. Then he rolled her over, his hands hard on her shoulders, and said only three words. "Who did it?"

Michelle was white, frozen by the look on his face. He looked deadly, his eyes cold and ferocious. He lifted her by the shoulders until she was almost nose to nose with him, and he repeated his question, the words evenly spaced, almost soundless. "Who did it?"

Her lips trembled as she looked helplessly at him. She couldn't talk about it; she just couldn't. "I don't ... It's noth—''

"Who did it?" he yelled, his neck corded with rage.

She closed her eyes, burning tears seeping from beneath her lids. Despair and shame ate at her, but she knew he wouldn't let her go until she answered. Her lips were trembling so hard she could barely talk. "John, please!"

"Who?"

Crumpling, she gave in, turning her face away. "Roger Beckman. My ex-husband." It was hard to say the words; she thought they would choke her.

John was swearing again, softly, endlessly. Michelle struggled briefly as he swept her up and sat down in a chair, holding her cradled on his lap, but it was a futile effort, so she abandoned it. Just saying Roger's name had made her feel unclean. She wanted to hide, to scrub herself over and over to be rid of the taint, but John wouldn't let her go. He held her naked on his lap, not saying a word after he'd stopped cursing until he noticed her shivering. The sun was hot, but her skin was cold. He stretched until he could reach the corner of the sheet, then jerked until it came free of the bed, and wrapped it around her.

He held her tight and rocked her, his hands stroking up and down her back. She'd been beaten. The knowledge kept ricocheting inside his skull, and he shook with a black rage he'd never known before. If he'd been able to get his hands on that slimy bastard right then, he'd have killed him with his bare hands and enjoyed every minute of it. He thought of Michelle cowering in fear and pain, her delicate body shuddering under the blows, and red mist colored his vision. No wonder she'd asked him not to hurt her the first time he'd made love to her! After her experience with men, it was something of a miracle that she'd responded at all.

He crooned to her, his rough cheek pressed against her sunny hair, his hard arms locked around her. He didn't know what he said, and neither did she, but the sound of his voice was enough. The gentleness came through, washing over her and warming her on the inside just as the heat of his body warmed her cold skin. Even after her shivering stopped he simply held her, waiting, letting her feel his closeness.

Finally she shifted a little, silently asking him to let her go. He did, reluctantly, his eyes never leaving her white face as she walked into the bathroom and shut the door. He started to go into the bathroom after her, alarmed by her silence and lack of color; his hand was on the doorknob when he reined himself under control. She needed to be alone right now. He heard the sound of the shower, and waited with unprecedented patience until she came out. She was still pale, but not as completely colorless as she'd been. The shower had taken the remaining chill from her skin, and she was wrapped in the terry-cloth robe she kept hanging on the back of the bathroom door.

"Are you all right?" he asked quietly.

"Yes." Her voice was muted.

"We have to talk about it."

"Not now." The look she gave him was shattered. "I can't. Not now."

"All right, baby. Later."

Later was that night, lying in his arms again, with the darkness like a shield around them. He'd made love to her, very gently and for a long time, easing her into rapture. In the lengthening silence afterward she felt his determination to know all the answers, and though she dreaded it, in the darkness she felt able to give them to him. When it came down to it, he didn't even have to ask. She simply started talking.

"He was jealous," she whispered. "Insane with it. I couldn't talk to a man at a party, no matter how ugly or happily married; I couldn't smile at a waiter. The smallest things triggered his rages. At first he'd just scream, accusing me of cheating on him, of loving someone else, and he'd ask me over and over who it was until I couldn't stand it anymore. Then he began slapping me. He was always sorry afterward. He'd tell me how much he loved me, swear he'd never do it again. But of course he did."

John had gone rigid, his muscles shaking with the rage she felt building in him again. In the darkness she stroked his face, giving him what comfort she could and never wondering at the illogic of it.

"I filed charges against him once; his parents bought him out of it and made it plain I wasn't to do such a thing again. Then I tried leaving him, but he found me and carried me back. He...he said he'd have Dad killed if I ever tried to leave him again."

"You believed him?" John asked harshly, the first words he'd spoken. She didn't flinch from the harshness, knowing it wasn't for her.

"Oh, yes, I believed him." She managed a sad little laugh. "I still do. His family has enough money that he could have it done and it would never be traced back to him."

"But you left him anyway."

"Not until I found a way to control him."

"How?"

She began trembling a little, and her voice wavered out of control. "The...the scars on my back. When he did that, his parents were in Europe; they weren't there to have files destroyed and witnesses bribed until it was too late. I already had a copy of everything, enough to press charges against him. I bought my divorce with it, and I made his parents promise to keep him away from me or I'd use what I had. They were very conscious of their position and family prestige.''

"Screw their prestige,'' he said flatly, trying very hard to keep his rage under control.

"It's academic now; they're dead.''

He didn't think it was much of a loss. People who cared more about their family prestige than about a young woman being brutally beaten and terrorized didn't amount to much in his opinion.

Silence stretched, and he realized she wasn't going to add anything else. If he let her, she'd leave it at that highly condensed and edited version, but he needed to know more. It hurt him in ways he'd never thought he could be hurt, but it was vital to him that he know all he could about her, or he would never be able to close the distance between them. He wanted to know where she went in her mind and why she wouldn't let him follow, what she was thinking, what had happened in the two years since her divorce.

He touched her back, caressing her with his fingertips. "Is this why you wouldn't go swimming?''

She stirred against his shoulder, her voice like gossamer wings in the darkness. "Yes. I know the scars aren't bad; they've faded a lot. But in my mind they're still like they were.... I was so scared someone would see them and ask how I got them.''

"That's why you always put your nightgown back on after we'd made love.''

She was silent, but he felt her nod.

"Why didn't you want *me* to know? I'm not exactly some stranger walking down the street."

No, he was her heart and her heartbreaker, the only man she'd ever loved, and therefore more important to her than anyone else in the world. She hadn't wanted him to know the ugliness that had been in her life.

"I felt dirty," she whispered. "Ashamed."

"Good God!" he exploded, raising up on his elbow to lean over her. "Why? It wasn't your fault. You were the victim, not the villain."

"I know, but sometimes knowledge doesn't help. The feelings were still there."

He kissed her, long and slow and hot, loving her with his tongue and letting her know how much he desired her. He kissed her until she responded, lifting her arms up to his neck and giving him her tongue in return. Then he settled onto the pillow again, cradling her head on his shoulder. She was nude; he had gently but firmly refused to let her put on a gown. That secret wasn't between them any longer, and she was glad. She loved the feel of his warm, hard-muscled body against her bare skin.

He was still brooding, unable to leave it alone. She felt his tension and slowly ran her hand over his chest, feeling the curly hair and small round nipples with their tiny center points. "Relax," she murmured, kissing his shoulder. "It's over."

"You said his parents controlled him, but they're dead. Has he bothered you since?"

She shivered, remembering the phone calls she'd had from Roger. "He called me a couple of times, at the house. I haven't seen him. I hope I never have to see him again." The last sentence was full of desperate sincerity.

"At the house? Your house? How long ago?"

"Before you brought me here."

"I'd like to meet him," John said quietly, menacingly.

"I hope you never do. He's... not sane."

They lay together, the warm, humid night wrapped around them, and she began to feel sleepy. Then he touched her again, and she felt the raw anger in him, the savage need to know. "What did he use?"

She flinched away from him. Swearing softly, he caught her close. "Tell me."

"There's no point in it."

"I want to know."

"You already know." Tears stung her eyes. "It isn't original."

"A belt."

Her breath caught in her throat. "He...he wrapped the leather end around his hand."

John actually snarled, his big body jerking. He thought of a belt buckle cutting into her soft skin, and it made him sick. It made him murderous. More than ever, he wanted to get his hands on Roger Beckman.

He felt her hands on him, clinging. "Please," she whispered. "Let's go to sleep."

He wanted to know one more thing, something that struck him as odd. "Why didn't you tell your dad? He had a lot of contacts; he could have done something. You didn't have to try to protect him."

Her laugh was soft and faintly bitter, not really a laugh at all. "I did tell him. He didn't believe me. It was easier for him to think I'd made it all up than to admit my life had gone so wrong."

She didn't tell him that she'd never loved Roger, that her life had gone wrong because she'd married one man while loving another.

Chapter 10

Telephone, Michelle!" Edie called from the kitchen.

Michelle had just come in, and she was on her way upstairs to shower; she detoured into the office to take the call there. Her mind was on her cattle; they were in prime condition, and John had arranged the sale. She would soon be leaving the ranks of the officially broke and entering those of the merely needy. John had scowled when she'd told him that.

"Hello," she said absently.

Silence.

The familiar chill went down her spine. "Hello!" she almost yelled, her fingers turning white from pressure.

"Michelle."

Her name was almost whispered, but she heard it, recognized it. "No," she said, swallowing convulsively. "Don't call me again."

"How could you do this to me?"

"Leave me alone!" she screamed, and slammed the phone down. Her legs were shaking, and she leaned on the desk, gulping in air. She was frightened. How had Roger found her here? Dear God, what would John do if he found out Roger was bothering her? He'd be furious.... More than furious. He'd be murderous. But what if Roger called again and John answered? Would Roger ask for her, or would he remain silent?

The initial silence haunted her, reminding her of the other phone calls she had received. She'd had the same horrible feeling from all of them. Then she knew: Roger had made those other phone calls. She couldn't begin to guess why he hadn't spoken, but suddenly she had no doubt about who her caller had been. Why hadn't she realized it before? He had the resources to track her down, and he was sick and obsessive enough to do so. He knew where she was, knew she was intimately involved with another man. She felt nauseated, thinking of his jealous rages. He was entirely capable of coming down here to snatch her away from the man he would consider his rival and take her back "where she belonged."

More than two years, and she still wasn't free of him.

She thought about getting an injunction against him for harassment, but John would have to know, because the telephone was his. She didn't want him to know; his reaction could be too violent, and she didn't want him to get in any trouble.

She wasn't given the option of keeping it from him. He opened the door to the office, a questioning look on his face as he stepped inside; Edie must have told him Michelle had a call, and that was unusual enough to make him curious. Michelle didn't have time to compose her face. He stopped, eyeing her sharply. She knew she looked pale and distraught. She watched as his eyes went slowly, inevitably, to the telephone. He never missed a detail, damn him; it was almost impossible to hide anything from him. She could have done it if she'd had time to deal with the shock, but now all she could do was stand frozen in her tracks. Why couldn't he have remained in the stable five minutes longer? She would have been in the shower; she would have had time to think of something.

"That was him, wasn't it?" he asked flatly.

Her hand crept toward her throat as she stared at him like a rabbit in a snare. John crossed the room with swift strides, catching her shoulders in his big warm hands.

"What did he say? Did he threaten you?"

Numbly she shook her head. "No. He didn't threaten me. It wasn't what he said; it's just that I can't stand hearing—" Her voice broke, and she tried to turn away, afraid to push her self-control any further.

John caught her more firmly to him, tucking her in the crook of one arm as he picked up the receiver. "What's his number?" he snapped.

Frantically Michelle tried to take the phone from him. "No, don't! That won't solve anything!"

His face grim, he evaded her efforts and pinned her arms to her sides. "He's good at terrorizing a woman, but it's time he knows there's someone else he'll have to deal with if he ever calls you again. Do you still remember his number or not? I can get it, but it'll be easier if you give it to me."

"It's unlisted," she said, stalling.

He gave her a long, level look. "I can get it," he repeated.

She didn't doubt that he could. When he decided to do something, he did it, and lesser people had better get out of his way. Defeated, she gave him the number and watched as he punched the buttons.

As close to him as she was, she could hear the ringing on the other end of the line, then a faint voice as someone answered. "Get Roger Beckman on the line," he ordered in the hard voice that no one disobeyed.

His brows snapped together in a scowl as he listened, then he said "Thanks" and hung up. Still frowning, he held her to him for a minute before telling her, "The housekeeper said he's on vacation in the south of France, and she doesn't know when he'll be back."

"But I just talked to him!" she said, startled. "He wasn't in France!"

John let her go and walked around to sit behind the desk, the frown turning abstracted. "Go on and take a shower," he said quietly. "I'll be up in a few minutes."

Michelle drew back, feeling cold all over again. Didn't he believe her? She knew Roger wasn't in the south of France; that call certainly hadn't been an overseas call. The connection had been too good, as clear as a local call. No, of course he didn't believe her, just as he hadn't believed her about the blue Chevrolet. She walked away, her back rigid and her eyes burning. Roger wasn't in France, even if the housekeeper had said he was, but why was he trying to keep his location a secret?

* * *

After Michelle left, John sat in the study, pictures running through his mind, and he didn't like any of them. He saw Michelle's face, so white and pinched, her eyes terrified; he saw the small white scars on her back, remembered the sick look she got when she talked about her ex-husband. She'd worn the same look just now. Something wasn't right. He'd see Roger Beckman in hell before he let the man anywhere near Michelle again.

He needed information, and he was willing to use any means available to him to get it. Michelle meant more to him than anything else in the world.

Something had happened the summer before at his neighbor's house over on Diamond Bay, and his neighbor, Rachel Jones, had been shot. John had seen pure hell then, in the black eyes of the man who had held Rachel's wounded body in his arms. The man had looked as if the pain Rachel had been enduring had been ripping his soul out. At the time John hadn't truly understood the depths of the man's agony; at the time he'd still been hiding the truth of his own vulnerability from himself. Rachel had married her black-eyed warrior this past winter. Now John understood the man's anguish, because now he had Michelle, and his own life would be worthless without her.

He'd like to have Rachel's husband, Sabin, with him now, as well as the big blond man who had been helping them. Those two men had something wild about them, the look of predators, but they would understand his need to protect Michelle. They would gladly have helped him hunt Beckman down like the animal he was.

He frowned. They weren't here, but Andy Phelps was, and Phelps had been involved with that mess at Diamond Bay last summer. He looked up a number and punched the buttons, feeling the anger build in him as he thought of Michelle's terrified face. "Andy Phelps, please."

When the sheriff's deputy answered, John said, "Andy, this is Rafferty. Can you do some quiet investigating?"

Andy was a former D.E.A. agent, and, besides that, he had a few contacts it wasn't safe to know too much about. He said quietly, "What's up?"

John outlined the situation, then waited while Andy thought of the possibilities.

"Okay, Michelle says the guy calling her is her ex-husband, but his housekeeper says he's out of the country, right?"

"Yeah."

"Is she sure it's her ex?"

"Yes. And she said he wasn't in France."

"You don't have a lot to go on. You'd have to prove he was the one doing the calling before you could get an injunction, and it sounds as if he's got a good alibi."

"Can you find out if he's really out of the country? I don't think he is, but why would he pretend, unless he's trying to cover his tracks for some reason?"

"You're a suspicious man, Rafferty."

"I have reason to be," John said in a cold, even tone. "I've seen the marks he left on Michelle. I don't want him anywhere near her."

Andy's voice changed as he digested that information, anger and disgust entering his tone. "Like that, huh? Do you think he's in the area?"

"He's certainly not at his home, and we know he isn't in France. He's calling Michelle, scaring her to death. I'd say it's a possibility."

"I'll start checking. There are a few favors I can call in. You might put a tape on your phone, so if he calls back you'll have proof."

"There's something else," John said, rubbing his forehead. "Michelle had an accident a few weeks ago. She said someone ran her off the road, a guy in a blue Chevrolet. I didn't believe her, damn it, and neither did the deputy. No one saw anything, and we didn't find any paint on the car, so I thought someone might have gotten a little close to her and she panicked. But she said he turned around, came back and tried to hit her again."

"That's not your usual someone-ran-me-off-the-road tale," Andy said sharply. "Has she said anything else?"

"No. She hasn't talked about it at all."

"You're thinking it could be her ex-husband."

"I don't know. It might not have anything at all to do with the phone calls, but I don't want to take the chance."

"Okay, I'll check around. Keep an eye on her, and hook a tape recorder up to the phone."

John hung up and sat there for a long time, silently using every curse word he knew. Keeping an eye on her would be easy; she hadn't been off the ranch since the accident, hadn't even gone to check her own house. Now he knew why, and he damned himself and Roger Beckman with equal ferocity. If he'd only paid attention the night of the accident, they might have been able to track down the Chevrolet, but so much time had passed now that he doubted it would ever be found. At least Michelle hadn't connected Beckman with the accident, and John didn't intend to mention the possibility to her. She was scared enough as it was.

It infuriated him that he couldn't do anything except wait for Andy to get back to him. Even then, it might be a dead end. But if Beckman was anywhere in the area, John intended to pay him a visit and make damned certain he never contacted Michelle again.

Michelle bolted upright in bed, her eyes wide and her face chalky. Beside her, John stirred restlessly and reached for her, but didn't awaken. She lay back down, taking comfort in his nearness, but both her mind and her heart were racing.

It was Roger.

Roger had been driving the blue Chevrolet. Roger had tried to kill her. He wasn't in France at all, but here in Florida, biding his time and waiting to catch her out alone. She remembered the feeling she had had before the accident, as if someone were watching her with vile malice, the same feeling the phone calls had given her. She should have tied it all together before.

He'd found out about John. Michelle even knew how he'd found out. Bitsy Sumner, the woman she and John had met in Tampa when they'd gone down to have the deed drawn up, was the worst gossip in Palm Beach. It wouldn't have taken long for the news to work its way up to Philadelphia that Michelle Cabot was very snuggly with an absolute *hunk*, a gorgeous, macho rancher with bedroom eyes that made Bitsy feel so *warm*. Michelle could almost hear Bitsy on the telephone, embroidering her tale and laughing wickedly as she speculated about the sexy rancher.

Roger had probably convinced himself that Michelle would come back to him; she could still hear him whispering how much he loved her, that he'd make it up to her and show her how good it could be between them. He would have gone into a jealous rage when he found out about John. At last he had known who the other man was, confirming the suspicions he'd had all along.

His mind must have snapped completely. She remembered what he'd said the last time he had called: "How could you do this to me?"

She felt trapped, panicked by the thought that he was out there somewhere, patiently waiting to catch her alone. She couldn't go to the police; she had no evidence, only her intuition, and people weren't arrested on intuition. Besides, she didn't put a lot of faith in the police. Roger's parents had bought them off in Philadelphia, and now Roger controlled all those enormous assets. He had unlimited funds at his disposal; who knew what he could buy? He might even have hired someone, in which case she had no idea who to be on guard against.

Finally she managed to go to sleep, but the knowledge that Roger was nearby ate at her during the next few days, disturbing her rest and stealing her appetite away. Despite the people around her, she felt horribly alone.

She wanted to talk to John about it, but bitter experience made her remain silent. How could she talk to him when he didn't believe her about the phone calls or the accident? He had hooked a tape recorder up to the telephone, but he hadn't discussed it with her, and she hadn't asked any questions. She didn't want to know about it if he were only humoring her.

Things had become stilted between them since the last
time Roger had called, and she felt even less able to
approach him than she had before. Only in bed were
things the same; she had begun to fear that he was tiring of her, but he didn't seem tired of her in bed. His
lovemaking was still as hungry and frequent as before.

Abruptly, on a hot, sunny morning, she couldn't
stand it any longer. She had been pushed so far that
she had reached her limit. Even a rabbit will turn and
fight when it's cornered. She was tired of it all, so tired
that she sometimes felt she was dragging herself
through water. Damn Roger! What did she have to do
to get him out of her life? There had to be something.
She couldn't spend the rest of her days peering around
every corner, too terrified to even go to a grocery store.
It made her angry when she thought how she had let
him confine her as surely as if he'd locked her in a
prison, and beginning today she was going to do
something about it.

She still had the file that had won her a divorce; now
that his parents were dead the file didn't mean as
much, but it still meant something. It was docu-
mented proof that Roger had attacked her once before. If he would only call again, she would have his
call on tape, and perhaps she could get him to say
something damaging. This was Florida, not Philadelphia; that much money would always be influential,
but down here he wouldn't have the network of old
family friends to protect him.

But the file was in the safe at her house, and she
wanted it in her possession, at John's. She didn't feel
secure leaving it in an empty house, even though she
kept the door locked. The house could easily be bro-

ken into, and the safe was a normal household one; she doubted whether it would prove to be all that secure if anyone truly wanted to open it. If Roger somehow got the file, she'd have no proof at all. Those photographs and records couldn't be replaced.

Making up her mind, she told Edie she was going riding and ran out to the stables. It was a pleasant ride across the pastures to her ranch, but she didn't enjoy it as she normally would have, because of the knot of tension forming in her stomach. Roger had seen her the last time she'd been there, and she couldn't forget the terror she'd felt when she'd seen the blue Chevrolet bearing down on her.

She approached the house from the rear, looking around uneasily as she slid off the horse, but everything was normal. The birds in the trees were singing. Quickly she checked all the doors and windows, but they all seemed tight, with no signs of forced entry. Only then did she enter the house and hurry to the office to open the safe. She removed the manila envelope and checked the contents, breathing a sigh of relief that everything was undisturbed, then slid the envelope inside her shirt and re-locked the safe.

The house had been closed up for a long time; the air was hot and stuffy. She felt dizzy as she stood up, and her stomach moved queasily. She hurried outside to the back porch, leaning against the wall and gulping fresh air into her lungs until her head cleared and her stomach settled. Her nerves were shot. She didn't know how much longer she could stand it, but she had to wait. He would call again; she knew it. Until then, there was precious little she could do.

Everything was still calm, quiet. The horse nickered a welcome at her as she mounted and turned toward home.

The stableman came out to meet her as she rode up, relief plain on his face. "Thank God you're back," he said feelingly. "The boss is raising pure hell—excuse me, ma'am. Anyway, he's been tearing the place up looking for you. I'll get word to him that you're back."

"Why is he looking for me?" she asked, bewildered. She had told Edie that she was going riding.

"I don't know, ma'am." He took the horse's reins from her hands as she slid to the ground.

Michelle went into the house and sought out Edie. "What has John in such an uproar?" she asked.

Edie lifted her eyebrows. "I didn't get close enough to ask."

"Didn't you tell him I'd gone riding?"

"Yep. That's when he really blew up."

She thought something might have come up and he couldn't find the paperwork he needed on it, but when she checked the office everything looked just as it had when she'd left that morning. Taking the manila envelope from inside her shirt, she locked it inside John's safe, and only then did she feel better. She *was* safe here, surrounded by John's people.

A few minutes later she heard his truck come up the drive, and judging from its speed, his temper hadn't settled any. More curious than alarmed, she walked out to meet him as the truck skidded to a stop, the tires throwing up a spray of sand and gravel. John thrust the door open and got out, his rifle clutched in his hand. His face was tight, and black fire burned in his eyes as he strode toward her. "Where in hell have you been?" he roared.

Michelle looked at the rifle. "I was out riding."

He didn't stop when he reached her, but caught her arm and hauled her inside the house. "Out riding where, damn it? I've had everyone combing the place for you."

"I went over to the house." She was beginning to get a little angry herself at his manner, though she still didn't know what had set him off. She lifted her nose and gave him a cool look. "I didn't realize I had to ask permission to go to my own house."

"Well, honey bunch, you have to do exactly that," he snapped, replacing the rifle in the gun cabinet. "I don't want you going anywhere without asking me first."

"I don't believe I'm your prisoner," she said icily.

"Prisoner, hell!" He whirled on her, unable to forget the raw panic that had filled him when he hadn't been able to find her. Until he knew what was going on and where Roger Beckman was, he'd like to have her locked up in the bedroom for safekeeping. One look at her outraged face, however, told him that he'd gone about it all wrong, and she was digging her heels in.

"I thought something had happened to you," he said more quietly.

"So you went tearing around the ranch looking for something to shoot?" she asked incredulously.

"No. I went tearing around the ranch looking for you, and I carried the rifle in case you were in any danger."

She balled her hands into fists, wanting to slap him. He wouldn't believe her about a real danger, but he was worried that she might sprain an ankle or take a tumble off a horse. "What danger could I possibly be in?" she snapped. "I'm sure there's not a snake on the ranch that would dare bite anything without your permission!"

His expression became rueful as he stared down at her. He lifted his hand and tucked a loose strand of sun-streaked hair behind her ear, but she still glared at him like some outraged queen. He liked her temper a lot better than the distant manner he'd been getting from her lately. "You're pretty when you're mad," he teased, knowing how that would get her.

For a moment she looked ready to spit. Then suddenly she sputtered, "You jackass," and began laughing.

He chuckled. No one could say "jackass" quite like Michelle, all hoity-toity and precise. He loved it. She could call him a jackass any time she wanted. Before she could stop laughing, he put his arms around her and hauled her against him, covering her mouth with his and slowly sliding his tongue between her lips. Her laughter stopped abruptly, her hands coming up to clutch his bulging biceps, and her tongue met his.

"You worried the hell out of me," he murmured when he lifted his mouth.

"Not all of it, I noticed," she purred, making him grin.

"But I wasn't kidding. I want to know whenever you go somewhere, and I don't want you going over to your place alone. It's been empty for quite a while, and a bum could start hanging around."

"What would a bum be doing this far out?" she asked.

"What would a bum be doing anywhere? Crime isn't restricted to cities. Please. For my peace of mind?"

It was so unusual for John Rafferty to plead for anything that she could only stare at him. It struck her that even though he'd said please, he still expected that she would do exactly as he'd said. In fact, she was only being perverse because he'd been his usual autocratic, arrogant self and made her angry. It suited her perfectly to be cautious, for the time being.

The dizziness and nausea she'd felt at the house must have been the beginning symptoms of some sort of bug, because she felt terrible the next day. She spent most of the day in bed, too tired and sick to worry about anything else. Every time she raised her head, the awful dizziness brought on another attack of nausea. She just wanted to be left alone.

She felt marginally better the next morning, and managed to keep something in her stomach. John held her in his arms, worried about her listlessness. "If you aren't a lot better tomorrow, I'm taking you to a doctor," he said firmly.

"It's just a virus," she sighed. "A doctor can't do anything."

"You could get something to settle your stomach."

"I feel better today. What if you catch it?"

"Then you can wait on me hand and foot until I'm better," he said, chuckling at her expression of horror. He wasn't worried about catching it. He couldn't remember the last time he'd even had a cold.

She was much better the next day, and though she still didn't feel like riding around the ranch, she did spend the morning in the office, feeding information into the computer and catching up on the books. It would be easier if they had a bookkeeping program for the computer; she made a note to ask John about it.

Roger still hadn't called.

She balled her fist. She knew he was somewhere close by! How could she get him to come out of hiding? She could never live a normal life as long as she was afraid to leave the ranch by herself.

But perhaps that was what she would have to do. Obviously Roger had some way of watching the ranch; she simply couldn't believe the blue Chevrolet had been a coincidence, unconnected to Roger. He'd caught her off guard that time, but now she'd be looking for him. She had to draw him out.

When John came to the house for lunch, she had twisted her hair up and put on a bit of makeup, and she knew she looked a lot better. "I thought I'd go to town for a few things," she said casually. "Is there anything you need?"

His head jerked up. She hadn't driven at all since the accident, and now here she was acting as nonchalant about driving as if the accident had never happened at all. Before he had worried that she was so reluctant to go anywhere, but now he wanted her to stay close. "What things?" he asked sharply. "Where exactly are you going?"

Her brows lifted at his tone. "Shampoo, hair conditioner, things like that."

"All right." He made an impatient gesture. "Where are you going? What time will you be back?"

"Really, you missed your calling. You should have been a prison guard."

"Just tell me."

Because she didn't want him to deny her the use of the car, she said in a bored voice, "The drugstore, probably. I'll be back by three."

He looked hard at her, then sighed and thrust his fingers through his thick black hair. "Just be careful."

She got up from the table. "Don't worry. If I wreck the car again, I'll pay for the damages with the money from the cattle sale."

He swore as he watched her stalk away. Damn, what could he do now? Follow her? He slammed into the office and called Andy Phelps to find out if he had any information on Roger Beckman yet. All Andy had come up with was that no one by the name of Roger Beckman had been on a flight to France in the last month, but he might not have gone there directly. It took time to check everything.

"I'll keep trying, buddy. That's all I can do."

"Thanks. Maybe I'm worried over nothing, but maybe I'm not."

"Yeah, I know. Why take chances? I'll call when I get something."

John hung up, torn by the need to do something, anything. Maybe he should tell Michelle of his suspicions, explain why he didn't want her wandering around by herself. But as Andy had pointed out, he really had nothing to go on, and he didn't want to upset her needlessly. She'd had enough worry in her life. If he had his way, nothing would ever worry her again.

Michelle drove to town and made her purchases, steeling herself every time a car drew near. But nothing happened; she didn't see anything suspicious, not even at the spot where the Chevrolet had forced her off the road. Fiercely she told herself that she wasn't paranoid, she hadn't imagined it all. Roger was there, somewhere. She simply had to find him. But she wasn't brave at all, and she was shaking with nerves by the time she got back to the ranch. She barely made it upstairs to the bathroom before her stomach rebelled and she retched miserably.

She tried it again the next day. And the next. Nothing happened, except that John was in the foulest mood she could imagine. He never came right out and forbade her to go anywhere, but he made it plain he didn't like it. If she hadn't been desperate, she would have thrown the car keys in his face and told him what he could do with them.

Roger had been watching her at her house that day. Could it be that he was watching that road instead of the one leading to town? He wouldn't have seen her when she'd gone over to get the file from the safe because she had ridden in from the back rather than using the road. John had told her not to go to her house alone, but she wouldn't have to go to the house. All she had to do was drive by on the road . . . and if Roger was there, he would follow her.

Chapter 11

She had to be crazy; she knew that. The last thing she wanted was to see Roger, yet here she was trying to find him, even though she suspected he was trying to kill her. No, she wanted to find him *because* of that. She certainly didn't want to die, but she wanted this to be over. Only then could she lead a normal life.

She wanted that life to be with John, but she had never fooled herself that their relationship was permanent, and the mood he was in these days could herald the end of it. Nothing she did seemed to please him, except when they were in bed, but perhaps that was just a reflection of his intense sex drive and any woman would have done.

Her nerves were so raw that she couldn't even think of eating the morning she planned to go to the house, and she paced restlessly, waiting until she saw John get in his pickup and drive across the pastures. She hadn't wanted him to know she was going anywhere; he asked too many questions, and it was hard to hide anything from him. She would only be gone half an hour, anyway, because when it came down to it, she didn't have the courage to leave herself hanging out as bait. All she could manage was one quick drive by; then she would come home.

She listened to the radio in an effort to calm her nerves as she drove slowly down the narrow gravel road. It came as a shock that the third hurricane of the season, Hurricane Carl, had formed in the Atlantic and was meandering toward Cuba. She had completely missed the first two storms. She hadn't even noticed that summer had slid into early autumn, because the weather was still so hot and humid, perfect hurricane weather.

Though she carefully searched both sides of the road for any sign of a car tucked away under the trees, she didn't see anything. The morning was calm and lazy. No one else was on the road. Frustrated, she turned around to drive back to the house.

A sudden wave of nausea hit her, and she had to halt the car. She opened the door and leaned out, her stomach heaving even though it was empty and nothing came out. When the spasm stopped she leaned against the steering wheel, weak and perspiring. This had hung on far too long to be a virus.

She lay there against the steering wheel for a long time, too weak to drive and too sick to care. A faint breeze wafted into the open door, cooling her hot face, and just as lightly the truth eased into her mind.

If this was a virus, it was the nine-month variety.

She let her head fall back against the seat, and a smile played around her pale lips. Pregnant. Of course. She even knew when it had happened: the night John had come home from Miami. He had been making love to her when she woke up, and neither of them had thought of taking precautions. She had been so on edge she hadn't noticed that she was late.

John's baby. It had been growing inside her for almost five weeks. Her hand drifted down to her stomach, a sense of utter contentment filling her despite the miserable way she felt. She knew the problems this would cause, but for the moment those problems were distant, unimportant compared to the blinding joy she felt.

She began to laugh, thinking of how sick she'd been. She remembered reading in some magazine that women who had morning sickness were less likely to miscarry than women who didn't; if that were true, this baby was as secure as Fort Knox. She still felt like death warmed over, but now she was happy to feel that way.

"A baby," she whispered, thinking of a tiny, sweet-smelling bundle with a mop of thick black hair and melting black eyes, though she realized any child of John Rafferty's would likely be a hellion.

But she couldn't continue sitting in the car, which was parked more on the road than off. Shakily, hoping the nausea would hold off until she could get home, she put the car in gear and drove back to the ranch with painstaking caution. Now that she knew what was wrong, she knew what to do to settle her stomach. And she needed to make an appointment with a doctor.

Sure enough, her stomach quieted after she ate a meal of dry toast and weak tea. Then she began to think about the problems.

Telling John was the first problem and, to Michelle, the biggest. She had no idea how he would react, but she had to face the probability that he would not be as thrilled as she was. She feared he was getting tired of her anyway; if so, he'd see the baby as a burden, tying him to a woman he no longer wanted.

She lay on the bed, trying to sort out her tangled thoughts and emotions. John had a right to know about his child, and, like it or not, he had a responsibility to it. On the other hand, she couldn't use the baby to hold him if he wanted to be free. Bleak despair filled her whenever she tried to think of a future without John, but she loved him enough to let him go. Since their first day together she had been subconsciously preparing for the time when he would tell her that he didn't want her any longer. That much was clear in her mind.

But what if he decided that they should marry because of the baby? John took his responsibilities seriously, even to the point of taking a wife he didn't want for the sake of his child. She could be a coward and grab for anything he offered, on the basis that the crumbs of affection that came her way would be better than nothing, or she could somehow find the courage to deny herself the very thing she wanted most. Tears filled her eyes, the tears that came so easily these days. She sniffled and wiped them away.

She couldn't decide anything; her emotions were see-sawing wildly between elation and depression. She didn't know how John would react, so any plans she made were a waste of time. This was something they would have to work out together.

She heard someone ride up, followed by raised, excited voices outside, but cowboys were always coming and going at the ranch, and she didn't think anything of it until Edie called upstairs, "Michelle? Someone's hurt. The boys are bringing him in— My God, it's the boss!" She yelled the last few words and Michelle shot off the bed. Afterward she never remembered running down the stairs; all she could remember was Edie catching her at the front door as Nev and another man helped John down from a horse. John was holding a towel to his face, and blood covered his hands and arms, and soaked his shirt.

Michelle's face twisted, and a thin cry burst from her throat. Edie was a big, strong woman, but somehow Michelle tore free of her clutching arms and got to John. He shrugged away from Nev and caught Michelle with his free arm, hugging her to him. "I'm all right," he said gruffly. "It looks worse than it is."

"You'd better get to a doc, boss," Nev warned. "Some of those cuts need stitches."

"I will. Get on back to the men and take care of things." John gave Nev a warning look over Michelle's head, and though one eye was covered with the bloody towel, Nev got the message. He glanced quickly at Michelle, then nodded.

"What happened?" Michelle cried frantically as she helped John into the kitchen. His arm was heavy around her shoulders, which told her more than anything that he was hurt worse than he wanted her to know. He sank onto one of the kitchen chairs.

"I lost control of the truck and ran into a tree," he muttered. "My face hit the steering wheel."

She put her hand on the towel to keep it in place, feeling him wince even under her light touch, and lifted his hand away. She could see thin shards of glass shining in the black depths of his hair.

"Let me see," she coaxed, and eased the towel away from his face.

She had to bite her lip to keep from moaning. His left eye was already swollen shut, and the skin on his cheekbone was broken open in a jagged wound. His cheekbone and brow ridge were already purple and turning darker as they swelled almost visibly, huge knots distorting his face. A long cut slanted across his forehead, and he was bleeding from a dozen other smaller cuts. She took a deep breath and schooled her voice to evenness. "Edie, crush some ice to go on his eye. Maybe we can keep the swelling from getting any worse. I'll get my purse and the car keys."

"Wait a minute," John ordered. "I want to clean up a little; I've got blood and glass all over me."

"That isn't important—"

"I'm not hurt that badly," he interrupted. "Help me out of this shirt."

When he used that tone of voice, he couldn't be budged. Michelle unbuttoned the shirt and helped him out of it, noticing that he moved with extreme caution. When the shirt was off, she saw the big red welt across his ribs and knew why he was moving so carefully. In a few hours he would be too sore to move at all. Easing out of the chair, he went to the sink and washed off the blood that stained his hands and arms, then stood patiently while Michelle took a wet cloth and gently cleaned his chest and throat, even his back. His hair was matted with blood on the left side, but she didn't want to try washing his head until he'd seen a doctor.

She ran upstairs to get a clean shirt for him and helped him put it on. Edie had crushed a good amount of ice and folded it into a clean towel to make a cold pad. John winced as Michelle carefully placed the ice over his eye, but he didn't argue about holding it in place.

Her face was tense as she drove him to the local emergency care clinic. He was hurt. It staggered her, because somehow she had never imagined John as being vulnerable to anything. He was as unyielding as granite, somehow seeming impervious to fatigue, illness or injury. His battered, bloody face was testimony that he was all too human, though, being John, he wasn't giving in to his injuries. He was still in control.

He was whisked into a treatment room at the clinic, where a doctor carefully cleaned the wounds and stitched the cut on his forehead. The other cuts weren't severe enough to need stitches, though they were all cleaned and bandaged. Then the doctor spent a long time examining the swelling around John's left eye. "I'm going to have you admitted to a hospital in Tampa so an eye specialist can take a look at this," he told John.

"I don't have time for a lot of poking," John snapped, sitting up on the table.

"It's your sight," the doctor said evenly. "You took a hell of a blow, hard enough to fracture your cheekbone. Of course, if you're too busy to save your eyesight—"

"He'll go," Michelle interrupted.

John looked at her with one furious black eye, but she glared back at him just as ferociously. There was something oddly magnificent about her, a difference he couldn't describe because it was so subtle. But even as pale and strained as she was, she looked good. She always looked good to him, and he'd be able to see her a lot better with two eyes than just one.

He thought fast, then growled, "All right." Let her think what she wanted about why he was giving in; the hard truth was that he didn't want her anywhere near the ranch right now. If he went to Tampa, he could insist that she stay with him, which would keep her out of harm's way while Andy Phelps tracked down whoever had shot out his windshield. What had been a suspicion was now a certainty as far as John was concerned; Beckman's threat went far beyond harassing telephone calls. Beckman had tried to make it look like an accident when he had run Michelle off the road, but now he had gone beyond that; a bullet wasn't accidental.

Thank God Michelle hadn't been with him as she usually was. At first he'd thought the bullet was intended for him, but now he wasn't so certain. The bullet had been too far to the right. Damn it, if only he hadn't lost control of the truck when the windshield shattered! He'd jerked the wheel instinctively, and the truck had started sliding on the dewy grass, hitting a big oak head-on. The impact had thrown him forward, and his cheekbone had hit the steering wheel with such force that he'd been unconscious for a few minutes. By the time he'd recovered consciousness and his head had cleared, there had been no point in sending any of his men to investigate where the shot had come from. Beckman would have been long gone, and they would only have destroyed any signs he might have left. Andy Phelps could take over now.

"I'll arrange for an ambulance," the doctor said, turning to leave the room.

"No ambulance. Michelle can take me down there."

The doctor sighed. "Mr. Rafferty, you have a concussion; you should be lying down. And in case of damage to your eye, you shouldn't strain, bend over, or be jostled. An ambulance is the safest way to get you to Tampa."

John scowled as much as he could, but the left side of his face was so swollen that he couldn't make the muscles obey. No way was he going to let Michelle drive around by herself in the Mercedes; the car would instantly identify her to Beckman. If he had to go to Tampa, she was going to be beside him every second. "Only if Michelle rides in the ambulance with me."

"I'll be right behind," she said. "No, wait. I need to go back home first, to pick up some clothes for both of us."

"No. Doc, give me an hour. I'll have clothes brought out to us and arrange for the car to be driven back to the house." To Michelle he said, "You either ride with me, or I don't go at all."

Michelle stared at him in frustration, but she sensed he wasn't going to back down on this. He'd given in surprisingly easy about going to the hospital, only to turn oddly stubborn about keeping her beside him. If someone drove the car back to the ranch, they would be stranded in Tampa, so it didn't make sense. This entire episode seemed strange, but she didn't know just why and didn't have time to figure it out. If she had to ride in an ambulance to get John to Tampa, she'd do it. She was still so scared and shocked by his accident that she would do anything to have him well again.

He took her acquiescence for granted, telling her what he wanted and instructing her to have Nev bring the clothes, along with another man to drive the car home. Mentally she threw her hands up and left the room to make the phone call. John waited a few seconds after the door had closed behind her, then said, "Doc, is there another phone I can use?"

"Not in here, and you shouldn't be walking around. You shouldn't even be sitting up. If the call is so urgent it won't wait, let your wife make it for you."

"I don't want her to know about it." He didn't bother to correct the doctor's assumption that Michelle was his wife. The good doctor was a little premature, that was all. "Do me a favor. Call the sheriff's department, tell Andy Phelps where I am and that I need to talk to him. Don't speak to anyone except Phelps."

The doctor's eyes sharpened, and he looked at the big man for a moment. Anyone else would have been flat on his back. Rafferty should have been, but his system must be like iron. He was still steady, and giving orders with a steely authority that made it almost impossible not to do as he said.

"All right, I'll make the call if you'll lie down. You're risking your eyesight, Mr. Rafferty. Think about being blind in that eye for the rest of your life."

John's lips drew back in a feral grin that lifted the corners of his mustache. "Then the damage has probably already been done, doctor." Losing the sight in his left eye didn't matter much when stacked against Michelle's life. Nothing was more important than keeping her safe.

"Not necessarily. You may not even have any damage to your eye, but with a blow that forceful it's better to have it checked. You may have what's called a blowout fracture, where the shock is transmitted to the wall of the orbital bone, the eye socket. The bone is thin, and it gives under the pressure, taking it away from the eyeball itself. A blowout fracture can save your eyesight, but if you have one you'll need surgery to repair it. Or you can have nerve damage, a dislocated lens, or a detached retina. I'm not an eye specialist, so I can't say. All I can tell you is to stay as quiet as possible or you can do even greater damage."

Impatiently John lay down, putting his hands behind his head, which was throbbing. He ignored the pain, just as he ignored the numbness of his face. Whatever damage had been done, was done. So he'd broken his cheekbone and maybe shattered his eye socket; he could live with a battered face or with just one good eye, but he couldn't live without Michelle.

He went over the incident again and again in his mind, trying to pull details out of his subconscious. In that split second before the bullet had shattered the windshield, had he seen a flash that might pinpoint Beckman's location? Had Beckman been walking? Not likely. The ranch was too big for a man to cover on foot. Nor was it likely he would have been on horseback; riding horses were harder to come by than cars, which could easily be rented. Going on the assumption that Beckman had been driving, what route could he have taken that would have kept him out of sight?

Andy Phelps arrived just moments before Nev. For Michelle's benefit, the deputy joked about John messing up his pretty face, then waited while John gave Nev detailed instructions. Nev nodded, asking few questions. Then John glanced at Michelle. "Why don't you check the things Nev brought; if you need anything else, he can bring it to Tampa."

Michelle hesitated for a fraction of a second, feeling both vaguely alarmed and in the way. John wanted her out of the room for some reason. She looked at the tall, quiet deputy, then back at John, before quietly leaving the room with Nev. Something was wrong; she knew it.

Even Nev was acting strangely, not quite looking her in the eye. Something had happened that no one wanted her to know, and it involved John.

He had given in too easily about going to the hospital, though the threat of losing his eyesight was certainly enough to give even John pause; then he had been so illogical about the car. John was never illogical. Nev was uneasy about something, and now John wanted to talk privately to a deputy. She was suddenly certain the deputy wasn't there just because he'd heard a friend was hurt.

Too many things didn't fit. Even the fact that John had had an accident at all didn't fit. He'd been driving across rough pastures since boyhood, long before he'd been old enough to have a driver's license. He was also one of the surest drivers she had ever seen, with quick reflexes and eagle-eyed attention to every other driver on the road. It just didn't make sense that he would lose control of his truck and hit a tree. It was too unlikely, too pat, too identical to her own accident.

Roger.

What a fool she had been! She had considered him as a danger only to herself, not to John. She should have expected his insane jealousy to spill over onto the man he thought had taken her away from him. While she had been trying to draw him out, he had been stalking John. Fiercely her hands knotted into fists.

Roger wouldn't stand a chance against John in an open fight, but he would sneak around like the coward he was, never taking the chance of a face-to-face confrontation.

She looked down at the two carryons Edie had packed for them and put her hand to her head. "I feel a little sick, Nev," she whispered. "Excuse me, I have to get to the restroom."

Nev looked around, worry etched on his face. "Do you want me to get a nurse? You do look kinda green."

"No, I'll be all right." She managed a weak smile as she lied, "I never have been able to stand the sight of blood, and it just caught up with me."

She patted his arm and went around the partition to the public restrooms, but didn't enter. Instead she waited a moment, sneaking peeks around the edge of the partition; as soon as Nev turned to sit down while waiting for her, she darted across the open space to the corridor where the examining rooms were. The door to John's room was closed, but not far enough for the latch to catch. When she cautiously nudged it, the door opened a crack. It was on the left side of the room, so John wouldn't be able to see it. Phelps should be on John's right side, facing him; with luck, he wouldn't notice the slight movement of the door, either.

Their voices filtered through the crack.

"—think the bullet came from a little rise just to the left of me," John said. "Nev can show you."

"Is there any chance the bullet could be in the upholstery?"

"Probably not. The trajectory wasn't angled enough."

"Maybe I can find the cartridge. I'm coming up with a big zero from the airlines, but I have another angle I can check. If he flew in, he'd have come in at Tampa, which means he'd have gotten his rental car at the airport. If I can get a match on his description, we'll have his license plate number."

"A blue Chevrolet. That should narrow it down," John said grimly.

"I don't even want to think about how many blue Chevrolets there are in this state. It was a good idea to keep Michelle with you in Tampa; it'll give me a few days to get a lead on this guy. I can get a buddy in Tampa to put surveillance on the hospital, if you think you'll need it."

"He won't be able to find her if the doctor here keeps quiet and if my file is a little hard to find."

"I can arrange that." Andy chuckled.

Michelle didn't wait to hear more. Quietly she walked back down the corridor and rejoined Nev. He was reading a magazine and didn't look up until she sat down beside him. "Feeling better?" he asked sympathetically.

She gave some answer, and it must have made sense, because it satisfied him. She sat rigidly in the chair, more than a little stunned. What she had overheard had verified her suspicion that Roger was behind John's "accident," but it was hard for her to take in the rest of it. John not only believed her about the phone calls, he had tied them in to the blue Chevrolet and had been quietly trying to track Roger down. That explained why he had suddenly become so insistent that she tell him exactly where she was going and how long she would be there, why he didn't want her going anywhere at all. He had been trying to protect her, while she had been trying to bait Roger into the open.

She hadn't told him what she was doing because she hadn't thought he would believe her; she had learned well the bitter lesson that she could depend only on herself, perhaps learned it too well. Right from the beginning John had helped her, sometimes against her will. He had stepped in and taken over the ranch chores that were too much for her; he was literally carrying her ranch until she could rebuild it into a profitable enterprise. He had given her love, comfort, care and concern, and now a child, but still she hadn't trusted him. He hadn't been tiring of her; he'd been under considerable strain to protect her.

Being John, he hadn't told her of his suspicions or what he was doing because he hadn't wanted to "worry" her. It was just like him. That protective, possessive streak of his was bone deep and body wide, defying logical argument. There were few things or people in his life that he cared about, but when he did care, he went full measure. He had claimed her as his, and what was his, he kept.

Deputy Phelps stopped by to chat; Michelle decided to give him an opportunity to talk to Nev, and she walked back to John's room. The ambulance had just arrived, so she knew they would be leaving soon.

When the door opened, he rolled his head until he could see her with his right eye. "Is everything okay?"

She had to grit her teeth against the rage that filled her when she saw his battered, discolored face. It made her want to destroy Roger in any way she could. The primitive, protective anger filled her, pumping into every cell in her body. It took every bit of control she had to calmly walk over to him as if she weren't in a killing rage and take his hand. "If you're all right, then I don't care what Edie packed or didn't pack."

"I'll be all right." His deep voice was confident. He might or might not lose the sight in his eye, but he'd be all right. John Rafferty was made of the purest, hardest steel.

She sat beside him in the ambulance and held his hand all the way to Tampa, her eyes seldom leaving his face. Perhaps he dozed; perhaps it was simply less painful if he kept his right eye closed, too. For whatever reason, little was said during the long ride.

It wasn't until they reached the hospital that he opened his eye and looked at her, frowning when he saw how drawn she looked. She needed the bed rest more than he did; if it hadn't been for his damned eye, and the opportunity to keep Michelle away from the ranch, he would already have been back at work.

He should have gotten her away when he'd first suspected Beckman was behind her accident, but he'd been too reluctant to let her out of his sight. He wasn't certain about her or how much she needed him, so he'd kept her close at hand. But the way she had looked when she saw he was hurt . . . a woman didn't look like that unless she cared. He didn't know how much she cared, but for now he was content with the fact that she did. He had her now, and he wasn't inclined to let go. As soon as this business with Beckman was settled, he'd marry her so fast she wouldn't know what was happening.

Michelle went through the process of having him admitted to the hospital while he was whisked off, with three—*three!*—nurses right beside him. Even as battered as he was, he exuded a masculinity that drew women like a magnet.

She didn't see him again for three hours. Fretting, she wandered the halls until a bout of nausea drove her to find the cafeteria, where she slowly munched on stale crackers. Her stomach gradually settled. John would probably be here for at least two days, maybe longer; how could she hide her condition from him when she would be with him practically every hour of the day? Nothing escaped his attention for long, whether he had one good eye or two. Breeding wasn't anything new to him; it was his business. Cows calved; mares foaled. On the ranch, everything mated and reproduced. It wouldn't take long for him to discard the virus tale she'd told him and come up with the real reason for her upset stomach.

What would he say if she told him? She closed her eyes, her heart pounding wildly at the thought. He deserved to know. She wanted him to know; she wanted to share every moment of this pregnancy with him. But what if it drove him to do something foolish, knowing that Roger not only threatened her but their child as well?

She forced herself to think clearly. They were safe here in the hospital; this was bought time. He wouldn't leave the hospital when staying here meant that she was also protected. She suspected that was the only reason he'd agreed to come at all. He was giving Deputy Phelps time to find Roger, if he could.

But what if Phelps hadn't found Roger by the time John left the hospital? What evidence did they have against him, anyway? He had had time to have any damage to the Chevrolet repaired, and no one had seen him shoot at John. He hadn't threatened her during any of those phone calls. He hadn't had to; she knew him, and that was enough.

She couldn't run, not any longer. She had run for two years, fleeing emotionally long after she had stopped physically running. John had brought her alive with his fierce, white-hot passion, forcing her out of her protective reserve. She couldn't leave him, especially now that she carried his child. She had to face Roger, face all the old nightmares and conquer them, or she would never be rid of this crippling fear. She could fight him, something she had always been too terrified to do before. She could fight him for John, for their baby, and she could damn well fight him for herself.

Finally she went back to the room that had been assigned to John to wait. It was thirty minutes more before he was wheeled into the room and transferred very carefully to the bed. When the door closed behind the orderlies he said, from between clenched teeth, "If anyone else comes through that door to do anything to me, I'm going to throw them out the window." Gingerly he eased into a more upright position against the pillow, then punched the button that raised the head of the bed.

She ignored his bad temper. "Have you seen the eye specialist yet?"

"Three of them. Come here."

There was no misreading that low demanding voice or the glint in his right eye as he looked at her. He held his hand out to her and said again, "Come here."

"John Patrick Rafferty, you aren't in any shape to begin carrying on like that."

"Aren't I?"

She refused to look at his lap. "You shouldn't be jostled."

"I don't want to be jostled. I just want a kiss." He gave her a slow, wicked grin despite the swelling in his face. "The spirit's willing, but the body's tired as hell."

She bent to kiss him, loving his lips gently with her own. When she tried to lift her head he thrust his fingers into her hair and held her down while his mouth molded to hers, his tongue making teasing little forays to touch hers. He gave a sigh of pleasure and let her up, but shifted his hand to her bottom to hold her beside him. "What've you been doing while I've been lying in cold halls in between bouts of being stuck, prodded, x-rayed and prodded some more?"

"Oh, I've been really entertained. You don't realize what an art mopping is until you've seen a master do it. There's also a four-star cafeteria here, specializing in the best stale crackers I've ever eaten." She grinned, thinking he'd never realize the truth of that last statement.

He returned the grin, thinking that once he would have accused her of being spoiled. He knew better now, because he'd been trying his damnedest to spoil her, and she persisted in being satisfied with far less than he would gladly have given her any day of the week. Her tastes didn't run to caviar or mink, and she'd been content to drive that old truck of hers instead of a Porsche. She liked silk and had beautiful clothes, but she was equally content wearing a cotton shirt and jeans. It wasn't easy to spoil a woman who was happy with whatever she had.

"Arrange to have a bed moved in here for you," he ordered. "Unless you want to sleep up here with me?"

"I don't think the nurses would allow that."

"Is there a lock on the door?"

She laughed. "No. You're out of luck."

His hand moved over her bottom, the slow, intimate touch of a lover. "We need to talk. Will it bother you if I lose this eye?"

Until then she hadn't realized that he might lose the eye as well as his sight. She sucked in a shocked breath, reaching blindly for his hand. He continued to watch her steadily, and slowly she relaxed, knowing what was important.

"It would bother me for your sake, but as for me… You can be one-eyed, totally blind, crippled, whatever, and I'll still love you."

There. She'd said it. She hadn't meant to, but the words had come so naturally that even if she could take them back, she wouldn't.

His right eye was blazing black fire at her. She had never seen anyone else with eyes as dark as his, night-black eyes that had haunted her from the first time she'd met him. She looked down at him and managed a tiny smile that was only a little hesitant as she waited for him to speak.

"Say that again."

She didn't pretend not to know what he meant, but she had to take another deep breath. Her heart was pounding. "I love you. I'm not saying that to try to trap you into anything. It's just the way I feel, and I don't expect you to—"

He put his fingers over her mouth. "It's about damn time," he said.

Chapter 12

You're very lucky, Mr. Rafferty," Dr. Norris said, looking over his glasses. "Your cheekbone seems to have absorbed most of the impact. It's fractured, of course, but the orbital bone is intact. Nor does there seem to be any damage to the eye itself, or any loss of sight. In other words, you have a hell of a shiner."

Michelle drew a deep breath of relief, squeezing John's hand. He winked at her with his right eye, then drawled, "So I've spent four days in a hospital because I have a black eye?"

Dr. Norris grinned. "Call it a vacation."

"Well, vacation's over, and I'm checking out of the resort."

"Just take it easy for the next few days. Remember that you have stitches in your head, your cheekbone is fractured, and you had a mild concussion."

"I'll keep an eye on him," Michelle said with a note of warning in her voice, looking at John very hard. He was probably planning to get on a horse as soon as he got home.

When they were alone again John put his hands behind his head, watching her with a distinct glitter in his eyes. After four days the swelling around his eye had subsided enough that he could open it a tiny slit, enough for him to see with it again. His face was still a mess, discolored in varying shades of black and purple, with a hint of green creeping in, but none of that mattered beside the fact that his eye was all right. "This has been a long four days," he murmured. "When we get home, I'm taking you straight to bed."

Her blood started running wild through her veins again, and she wondered briefly if she would always have this uncontrolled response to him. She'd been completely vulnerable to him from the start, and her reaction now was even stronger. Her body was changing as his baby grew within her, invisible changes as yet, but her skin seemed to be more sensitive, more responsive to his lightest touch. Her breasts throbbed slightly, aching for the feel of his hands and mouth.

She had decided not to tell him about the baby just yet, especially not while his eyesight was still in doubt, and had been at pains during the past four days to keep her uneasy stomach under control. She munched on crackers almost constantly, and had stopped drinking coffee because it made the nausea worse.

She could still see the hard satisfaction that had filled his face when she'd told him she loved him, but he hadn't returned the words. For a horrible moment she'd wondered if he was gloating, but he'd kissed her so hard and hungrily that she had dismissed the notion even though she'd felt a lingering pain. That night, after the lights were out and she was lying on the cot that had been brought in, he had said, "Michelle."

His voice was low, and he hadn't moved. She'd lifted her head to stare through the darkness at him. "Yes?"

"I love you," he had said quietly.

Tremors shook her, and tears leaped to her eyes, but they were happy tears. "I'm glad," she had managed to say.

He'd laughed in the darkness. "You little tease, just wait until I get my hands on you again."

"I can't wait."

Now he was all right, and they were going home. She called Nev to come pick them up, then hung up the phone with hands that had become damp. She wiped them on her slacks and lifted her chin. "Have you heard if Deputy Phelps has found a lead on Roger yet?"

John had been dressing, but at her words his head snapped around and his good eye narrowed on her. Slowly he zipped his jeans and fastened them, then walked around the bed to tower over her threateningly. Michelle's gaze didn't waver, nor did she lower her chin, even though she abruptly felt very small and helpless.

He didn't say anything, but simply waited, his mouth a hard line beneath his mustache. "I eavesdropped," she said calmly. "I had already made the connection between the phone calls and the guy who forced me off the road, but how did you tie everything together?''

"Just an uneasy feeling and a lot of suspicions," he said. "After that last call, I wanted to make certain I knew where he was. There were too many loose ends, and Andy couldn't find him on any airline's overseas passenger list. The harder Beckman was to find, the more suspicious it looked."

"You didn't believe me at first, about the blue Chevrolet."

He sighed. "No, I didn't. Not at first. I'm sorry. It was hard for me to face the fact that anyone would want to hurt you. But something was bothering you. You didn't want to drive, you didn't want to leave the ranch at all, but you wouldn't talk about it. That's when I began to realize you were scared."

Her green eyes went dark. "Terrified is a better word," she whispered, looking out the window. "Have you heard from Phelps?"

"No. He wouldn't call here unless he'd found Beckman."

She shivered, the strained look coming back into her face. "He tried to kill you. I should have known, I should have done something."

"What could you have done?" he asked roughly. "If you'd been with me that day, the bullet would have hit you, instead of just shattering the windshield."

"He's so jealous he's insane." Thinking of Roger made her feel sick, and she pressed her hand to her stomach. "He's truly insane. He probably went wild when I moved in with you. The first couple of phone calls, he didn't say anything at all. Maybe he had just been calling to see if I answered the phone at your house. He couldn't stand for me to even talk to any other man, and when he found out that you and I—'' She broke off, a fine sheen of perspiration on her face.

Gently John pulled her to him, pressing her head against his shoulder while he soothingly stroked her hair. "I wonder how he found out."

"Bitsy Sumner," Michelle said shakily.

"The airhead we met in the restaurant?"

"That airhead is the biggest gossip I know."

"If he's that far off his rocker, he probably thinks he's finally found the 'other man' after all these years."

She jumped, then gave a tight little laugh. "He has."

"What?" His voice was startled.

She eased away from him and pushed her hair back from her face with a nervous gesture. "It's always been you," she said in a low voice, looking anywhere except at him. "I couldn't love him the way I should have, and somehow he ... seemed to know it."

He put his hand on her chin and forced her head around. "You acted like you hated me, damn it."

"I had to have some protection from you." Her green eyes regarded him with a little bitterness. "You had women falling all over you, women with a lot more experience, and who were a lot prettier. I was only eighteen, and you scared me to death. People called you 'Stud!' I knew I couldn't handle a man like you, even if you'd ever looked at me twice."

"I looked," he said harshly. "More than twice. But you turned your nose up at me as if you didn't like my smell, so I left you alone, even though I wanted you so much my guts were tied in knots. I built that house for you, because you were used to a lot better than the old house I was living in. I built the swimming pool because you liked to swim. Then you married some fancy-pants rich guy, damn you, and I felt like tearing the place down stone by stone.''

Her lips trembled. ''If I couldn't have you, it didn't matter who I married.''

''You could have had me.''

''As a temporary bed partner? I was so young I thought I had to have it all or nothing. I wanted forever after, for better or worse, and your track record isn't that of a marrying man. Now...'' She shrugged, then managed a faint smile. ''Now all that doesn't matter.''

Hard anger crossed his face, then he said, ''That's what you think,'' and covered her mouth with his. She opened her lips to him, letting him take all he wanted. The time was long past when she could deny him anything, any part of herself. Even their kisses had been restrained for the past four days, and the hunger was so strong in him that it overwhelmed his anger; he kissed her as if he wanted to devour her, his strong hands kneading her flesh with barely controlled ferocity, and she reveled in it. She didn't fear his strength or his roughness, because they sprang from passion and aroused an answering need inside her.

Her nails dug into his bare shoulders as her head fell back, baring her throat for his mouth. His hips moved rhythmically, rubbing the hard ridge of his manhood against her as his self-control slipped. Only the knowledge that a nurse could interrupt them at any moment gave him the strength to finally ease away from her, his breath coming hard and fast. The way he felt now was too private, too intense, for him to allow even the chance of anyone walking in on them.

"Nev had better hurry," he said roughly, unable to resist one more kiss. Her lips were pouty and swollen from his kisses, her eyes half-closed and drugged with desire; that look aroused him even more, because he had put it there.

Michelle slipped out of the bedroom, her clothes in her hand. She didn't want to take a chance on waking John by dressing in the bedroom; he had been sleeping heavily since the accident, but she didn't want to push her luck. She had to find Roger. He had missed killing John once; he might not miss the second time. And she knew John; if he made even a pretense of following the doctor's order to take it easy, she'd be surprised. No, he would be working as normal, out in the open and vulnerable.

He had talked to Deputy Phelps the night before, but all Andy had come up with was that a blue Chevrolet had been rented to a man generally matching Roger's physical description, and calling himself Edward Walsh. The familiar cold chill had gone down Michelle's spine. "Edward is Roger's middle name," she had whispered. "Walsh was his mother's maiden name." John had stared at her for a long moment before relaying the information to Andy.

She wouldn't allow Roger another opportunity to hurt John. Oddly, she wasn't afraid for herself. She had already been through so much at Roger's hands that she simply couldn't be afraid any longer, but she was deathly afraid for John, and for this new life she carried. She couldn't let this go on.

Lying awake in the darkness, she had suddenly known how to find him. She didn't know exactly where he was, but she knew the general vicinity; all she had to do was bait the trap, and he would walk into it. The only problem was that she was the bait, and she would be in the trap with him.

She left a note for John on the kitchen table and ate a cracker to settle her stomach. To be on the safe side, she carried a pack of crackers with her as she slipped silently out the back door. If her hunch was right, she should be fairly safe until someone could get there. Her hand strayed to her stomach. She had to be right.

The Mercedes started with one turn of the ignition key, its engine smooth and quiet. She put it in gear and eased it down the driveway without putting on the lights, hoping she wouldn't wake Edie or any of the men.

Her ranch was quiet, the old house sitting silent and abandoned under the canopy of big oak trees. She unlocked the door and let herself in, her ears straining to hear every noise in the darkness. It would be dawn within half an hour; she didn't have much time to bait the trap and lure Roger in before Edie would find the note on the table and wake John.

Her hand shook as she flipped on the light in the foyer. The interior of the house jumped into focus, light and shadow rearranging themselves into things she knew as well as she knew her own face. Methodically she walked around, turning on the lights in the living room, then moving into her father's office, then the dining room, then the kitchen. She pulled the curtains back from the windows to let the lights shine through like beacons, which she meant them to be.

She turned on the lights in the laundry room, and in the small downstairs apartment used by the housekeeper a long time ago, when there had been a housekeeper. She went upstairs and turned on the lights in her bedroom, where John had taken her for the first time and made it impossible for her to ever be anything but his. Every light went on, both upstairs and downstairs, piercing the predawn darkness. Then she sat down on the bottom step of the stairs and waited. Soon someone would come. It might be John, in which case he would be furious, but she suspected it would be Roger.

The seconds slipped past, becoming minutes. Just as the sky began to take on the first gray tinge of daylight, the door opened and he walked in.

She hadn't heard a car, which meant she had been right in thinking he was close by. Nor had she heard his steps as he crossed the porch. She had no warning until he walked through the door, but, oddly, she wasn't startled. She had known he would be there.

"Hello, Roger," she said calmly. She had to remain calm.

He had put on a little weight in the two years since she had seen him, and his hair was a tad thinner, but other than that he looked the same. Even his eyes still looked the same, too sincere and slightly mad. The sincerity masked the fact that his mind had slipped, not far enough that he couldn't still function in society, but enough that he could conceive of murder and be perfectly logical about it, as if it were the only thing to do.

He carried a pistol in his right hand, but he held it loosely by the side of his leg. "Michelle," he said, a little confused by her manner, as if she were greeting a guest. "You're looking well." It was a comment dictated by a lifetime of having the importance of good manners drilled into him.

She nodded gravely. "Thank you. Would you like a cup of coffee?" She didn't know if there was any coffee in the house, and even if there were, it would be horribly stale, but the longer she could keep him off balance, the better. If Edie wasn't in the kitchen now, she would be in a few minutes, and she would wake John. Michelle hoped John would call Andy, but he might not take the time. She figured he would be here in fifteen minutes. Surely she could handle Roger for fifteen minutes. She thought the brightly lit house would alert John that something was wrong, so he wouldn't come bursting in, startling Roger into shooting. It was a chance, but so far the chances she had taken had paid off.

Roger was staring at her with a feverish glitter in his eyes, as if he couldn't look at her enough. Her question startled him again. "Coffee?"

"Yes. I think I'd like a cup, wouldn't you?" The very thought of coffee made her stomach roll, but making it would take time. And Roger was very civilized; he would see nothing wrong with sharing a cup of coffee with her.

"Why, yes. That would be nice, thank you."

She smiled at him as she got up from the stairs. "Why don't you chat with me while the coffee's brewing? I'm certain we have a lot of gossip to catch up on. I only hope I have coffee; I may have forgotten to buy any. It's been so hot this summer, hasn't it? I've become an iced-tea fanatic."

"Yes, it's been very hot," he agreed, following her into the kitchen. "I thought I might spend some time at the chalet in Colorado. It should be pleasant this time of year."

She found a half-empty pack of coffee in the cabinet; it was probably so stale it would be undrinkable, but she carefully filled the pot with water and poured it into the coffeemaker, then measured out the coffee into the paper filter. Her coffeemaker was slow; it took almost ten minutes to make a pot. The perking, hissing sounds it made were very soothing.

"Please sit down," she invited, indicating the chairs at the kitchen table.

Slowly he took a chair, then placed the pistol on the table. Michelle didn't let herself look at it as she turned to take two mugs from the cabinet. Then she sat down and took another cracker from the pack she had brought with her; she had left it on the table earlier, when she was going around the house turning on all the lights. Her stomach was rolling again, perhaps from tension as much as the effects of pregnancy.

"Would you like a cracker?" she asked politely.

He was watching her again, his eyes both sad and wild. "I love you," he whispered. "How could you leave me when I need you so much? I wanted you to come back to me. Everything would have been all right. I promised you it would be all right. Why did you move in with that brute rancher? *Why did you have to cheat on me like that?*"

Michelle jumped at the sudden lash of fury in his voice. His remarkably pleasant face was twisting in the hideous way she remembered in her nightmares. Her heart began thudding against her ribs so painfully that she thought she might be sick after all, but somehow she managed to say with creditable surprise, "But, Roger, the electricity had been disconnected. You didn't expect me to live here without lights or water, did you?"

Again he looked confused by the unexpected change of subject, but only momentarily. He shook his head. "You can't lie to me anymore, darling. You're still living with him. I just don't understand. I offered you so much more: all the luxury you could want, jewelry, shopping trips in Paris, but instead you ran away from me to live with a sweaty rancher who smells of cows."

She couldn't stop the coldness that spread over her when he called her "darling." She swallowed, trying to force back the panic welling in her. If she panicked, she wouldn't be able to control him. How many minutes did she have left? Seven? Eight?

"I wasn't certain you wanted me back," she managed to say, though her mouth was so dry she could barely form the words.

Slowly he shook his head. "You had to know. You just didn't want to come back. You *like* what that sweaty rancher can give you, when you could have lived like a queen. Michelle, darling, it's so sick for you to let someone like him touch you, but you enjoy it, don't you? It's *unnatural!*"

She knew all the signs. He was working himself into a frenzy, the rage and jealousy building in him until he lashed out violently. How could even Roger miss seeing why she would prefer John's strong, clean masculinity and earthy passions to his own twisted parody of love? How much longer would it be? Six minutes?

"I called your house," she lied, desperately trying to defuse his temper. "Your housekeeper said you were in France. I wanted you to come get me. I wanted to come back to you."

He looked startled, the rage draining abruptly from his face as if it had never been. He didn't even look like the same man. "You . . . you wanted . . ."

She nodded, noting that he seemed to have forgotten about the pistol. "I missed you. We had so much fun together, didn't we?" It was sad, but in the beginning they *had* had fun. Roger had been full of laughter and gentle teasing, and she had hoped he could make her forget about John.

Some of that fun was suddenly echoed in his eyes, in the smile that touched his mouth. "I thought you were the most wonderful thing I'd ever seen," he said softly. "Your hair is so bright and soft, and when you smiled at me, I felt ten feet tall. I would have given you the world. I would have killed for you." Still smiling, his hand moved toward the pistol.

Five minutes?

The ghost of the man he had been faded, and suddenly pity moved her. It wasn't until that moment that she understood Roger was truly ill; something in his mind had gone very wrong, and she didn't think all the psychiatrists or drugs in the world would be able to help him.

"We were so young," she murmured, wishing things could have been different for the laughing young man she had known. Little of him remained now, only moments of remembered fun to lighten his eyes. "Do you remember June Bailey, the little red-head who fell out of Wes Conlan's boat? We were all trying to help her back in, and somehow we all wound up in the water except for Toni. She didn't know a thing about sailing, so there she was on the boat, screaming, and we were swimming like mad, trying to catch up to her."

Four minutes.

He laughed, his mind sliding back to those sunny, goofy days.

"I think the coffee's about finished," she murmured, getting up. Carefully she poured two cups and carried them back to the table. "I hope you can drink it. I'm not much of a coffee-maker." That was better than telling him the coffee was stale because she had been living with John.

He was still smiling, but his eyes were sad. As she watched, a sheen of tears began to brighten his eyes, and he picked up the pistol. "I do love you so much," he said. "You never should have let that man touch you." Slowly the barrel came around toward her.

A lot of things happened simultaneously. The back door exploded inward, propelled by a kick that took it off the hinges. Roger jerked toward the sound and the pistol fired, the shot deafening in the confines of the house. She screamed and ducked as two other men leaped from the inside doorway, the biggest one taking Roger down with a tackle that sent him crashing into the table. Curses and shouts filled the air, along with the sound of wood splintering; then another shot assaulted her ears and strengthened the stench of cordite. She was screaming John's name over and over, knowing he was the one rolling across the floor with Roger as they both struggled for the gun. Then suddenly the pistol skidded across the floor and John was straddling Roger as he drove his fist into the other man's face.

The sickening thudding made her scream again, and she kicked a shattered chair out of her way, scrambling for the two men. Andy Phelps and another deputy reached them at the same time, grabbing John and trying to wrestle him away, but his face was a mask of killing fury at the man who had tried to murder his woman. He slung their hands away with a roar. Sobbing, Michelle threw her arms around his neck from behind, her shaking body against his back. "John, don't, please," she begged, weeping so hard that the words were almost unintelligible. "He's very sick."

He froze, her words reaching him as no one else's could. Slowly he let his fists drop and got to his feet, hauling her against him and holding her so tightly that she could barely breathe. But breathing wasn't important right then; nothing was as important as holding him and having him hold her, his head bent down to hers as he whispered a choked mixture of curses and love words.

The deputies had pulled Roger to his feet and cuffed his hands behind his back, while the pistol was put in a plastic bag and sealed. Roger's nose and mouth were bloody, and he was dazed, looking at them as if he didn't know who they were, or where he was. Perhaps he didn't.

John held Michelle's head pressed to his chest as he watched the deputies take Beckman out. God, how could she have been so cool, sitting across the kitchen table from that maniac and calmly serving him coffee? The man made John's blood run cold.

But she was safe in his arms now, the most precious part of his world. She had said a lot about his tomcatting reputation and the women in his checkered past; she had even called him a heartbreaker. But she was the true heartbreaker, with her sunlight hair and summer-green eyes, a golden woman who he never would have forgotten, even if she'd never come back into his life. Beckman had been obsessed with her, had gone mad when he lost her, and for the first time John thought he might understand. He wouldn't have a life, either, if he lost Michelle.

"I lost twenty years off my life when I found that note," he growled into her hair.

She clung to him, not loosening her grip. "You got here faster than I'd expected," she gasped, still crying a little. "Edie must've gotten up early."

"No, I got up early. You weren't in bed with me, so I started hunting you. As it was, we barely got here in time. Edie would have been too late."

Andy Phelps sighed, looking around the wrecked kitchen. Then he found another cup in the cabinet and poured himself some coffee. He made a face as he sipped it. "This stuff is rank. It tastes just like what we get at work. Anyway, I think I have my pajama bottoms on under my pants. When John called I took the time to dress, but I don't think I took the time to undress first."

They both looked at him. He still looked a little sleepy, and he certainly wasn't in uniform. He had on jeans, a T-shirt, and running shoes with no socks. He could have worn an ape suit for all she cared.

"I need both of you to make statements," he said. "But I don't think this will ever come to trial. From what I saw, he won't be judged mentally competent."

"No," Michelle agreed huskily. "He isn't."

"Do we have to make the statements right now?" John asked. "I want to take Michelle home for a while."

Andy looked at both of them. Michelle was utterly white, and John looked the worse for wear, too. He had to still be feeling the effects of hitting a steering wheel with his face. "No, go on. Come in sometime this afternoon."

John nodded and walked Michelle out of the house. He'd commandeered Nev's truck, and now he led her to it. Someone else could get the car later.

It was a short, silent drive back to the ranch. She climbed numbly out of the truck, unable to believe it was all over. John swung her up in his arms and carried her into the house, his hard arms tight around her. Without a word to anyone, even Edie, who watched them with lifted brows, he took her straight upstairs to their bedroom and kicked the door shut behind him.

He placed her on the bed as if she might shatter, then suddenly snatched her up against him again. "I could kill you for scaring me like that," he muttered, even though he knew he'd never be able to hurt her. She must have known it, too, because she cuddled closer against him.

"We're getting married right away," he ordered in a voice made harsh with need. "I heard part of what he said, and maybe he's right that I can't give you all the luxuries you deserve, but I swear to God I'll try to make you happy. I love you too much to let you go.''

"I've never said anything about going," Michelle protested. Married? He wanted to get married? Abruptly she lifted her head and gave him a glowing smile, one that almost stopped his breathing.

"You never said anything about staying, either.''

"How could I? This is your house. It was up to you.''

"Good manners be damned," he snapped. "I was going crazy, wondering if you were happy.''

"Happy? I've been sick with it. You've given me something that doesn't have a price on it." She lifted her nose at him. "I've heard that mingling red blood with blue makes very healthy babies.''

He looked down at her with hungry fire in his eyes. "Well, I hope you like babies, honey, because I plan on about four.''

"I like them very much," she said as she touched her stomach. "Even though this is making me feel really ghastly.''

For a moment he looked puzzled, then his gaze drifted downward. His expression changed to one of stunned surprise, and he actually paled a little. "You're pregnant?''

"Yes. Since the night you came back from your last trip to Miami.''

His right brow lifted as he remembered that night; the left side of his face was still too swollen for him to be able to move it much. Then a slow grin began to widen his mouth, lifting the corners of his mustache. "I was careless one time too many," he said with visible satisfaction.

She laughed. "Yes, you were. Were you trying to be?"

"Who knows?" he asked, shrugging. "Maybe. God knows I like the idea. How about you?"

She reached for him, and he pulled her onto his lap, holding her in his arms and loving the feel of her. She rubbed her face against his chest. "All I've ever wanted is for you to love me. I don't need all that expensive stuff; I like working on the ranch, and I want to build my own ranch up again, even after we're married. Having your baby is…just more of heaven."

He laid his cheek on her golden hair, thinking of the terror he'd felt when he'd read her note. But now she was safe, she was his, and he would never let her go. She'd never seen any man as married as he planned to be. He'd spend the rest of his life trying to pamper her, and she'd continue to calmly ignore his orders whenever the mood took her, just as she did now. It would be a long, peaceful life, anchored in hard work and happily shrieking kids.

It would be good.

Their wedding day dawned clear and sunny, though the day before Michelle had resigned herself to having the wedding inside. But Hurricane Carl, after days of meandering around like a lost bee, had finally decided to head west and the clouds had vanished, leaving behind a pure, deep blue sky unmarred by even a wisp of cloud.

Michelle couldn't stop smiling as she dressed. If there were any truth in the superstition that it was bad luck for the groom to see the bride on their wedding day, she and John were in for a miserable life, but somehow she just couldn't believe it. He had not only refused to let her sleep in another room the night before, he'd lost his temper over the subject. She was damn well going to sleep with him where she belonged, and that was that. Tradition could just go to hell as far as he was concerned, if it meant they had to sleep apart. She had noticed that he hadn't willingly let her out of his sight since the morning they had caught Roger, so she understood.

His rather calm acceptance of his impending fatherhood had been a false calm, one shock too many after a nerve-wracking morning. The reality of it had hit him during the night, and Michelle had awakened to find herself clutched tightly to his chest, his face buried in her hair and his muscled body shaking, while he muttered over and over, "A baby. My God, a baby." His hand had been stroking her stomach as if he couldn't quite imagine his child growing inside her slim body. It had become even more real to him the next morning when even crackers couldn't keep her stomach settled, and he had held her while she was sick.

Some mornings weren't bad at all, while some were wretched. This morning John had put a cracker in her mouth before she was awake enough to even open her eyes, so she had lain in his arms with her eyes closed, chewing on her "breakfast." When it became evident that this was going to be a good morning, the bridegroom had made love to the bride, tenderly, thoroughly, and at length.

They were even dressing together for their wedding. She watched as he fastened his cuff links, his hard mouth curved in a very male, very satisfied way.

He had found her lace teddy and garter belt extremely erotic, so much so that now they risked being late to their own wedding.

"I need help with my zipper when you've finished with that," she said.

He looked up, and a slow smile touched his lips, then lit his black eyes. "You look good enough to eat."

She couldn't help laughing. "Does this mean we'll have to reschedule the wedding for tomorrow?"

The smile became a grin. "No, we'll make this one." He finished his cuff links. "Turn around."

She turned, and his warm fingers touched her bare back, making her catch her breath and shiver in an echo of delight. He kissed her exposed nape, holding her as the shiver became a sensuous undulation. He wouldn't have traded being with her on this particular morning for all the tradition in the world.

Her dress was a pale, icy yellow, as was the garden hat she had chosen to wear. The color brought out the bright sunniness of her hair and made her glow, though maybe it wasn't responsible for the color in her cheeks or the sparkle in her eyes. That could be due to early pregnancy, or to heated lovemaking. Or maybe it was sheer happiness.

He worked the zipper up without snagging any of the delicate fabric, then bent to straighten and smooth her skirt. He shrugged into his jacket as she applied lipstick and carefully set the hat on her head. The yellow streamers flowed gracefully down her back. "Are we ready?" she asked, and for the first time he heard a hint of nervousness in her voice.

"We're ready," he said firmly, taking her hand. Their friends were all waiting on the patio; even his mother had flown up from Miami, a gesture that had surprised him but, on reflection, was appreciated.

Without the shadow of Roger Beckman hanging over her, Michelle had flowered in just these few days. Until she had made the effort to confront Roger, to do something about him once and for all, she hadn't realized the burden she'd been carrying around with her. Those black memories had stifled her spirit, made her wary and defensive, unwilling to give too much of herself. But she had faced him, and in doing so she had faced the past. She wasn't helpless any longer, a victim of threats and violence.

Poor Roger. She couldn't help feeling pity for him, even though he had made her life hell. At her insistence, John and Andy had arranged for Roger to have medical tests immediately, and it hadn't taken the doctors long to make a diagnosis. Roger had a slow but relentlessly degenerative brain disease. He would never be any better, and would slowly become worse until he finally died an early death, no longer knowing anyone or anything. She couldn't help feeling grief for him, because at one time he'd been a good, kind young man. She wished there were some help for him, but the doctors didn't hold out any hope.

John put his arm around her, seeing the shadows that had come into her eyes. He didn't share her sympathy for Beckman, though perhaps in time he would be able to forget the moment when that pistol had swung toward her. Maybe in a few centuries.

He tilted her head up and kissed her, taking care not to smear her lipstick. "I love you," he murmured.

The sun came back out in her eyes. "I love you, too."

He tucked her hand into the crook of his arm. "Let's go get married."

Together they walked down the stairs and out to the patio, where their friends waited and the sun shone down brightly, as if to apologize for the threat of a storm the day before. Michelle looked at the tall man by her side; she wasn't naive enough to think there wouldn't be storms in their future, because John's arrogance would always make her dig in her heels, but she found herself looking forward to the battles they would have. The worst was behind them, and if the future held rough weather and sudden squalls...well, what future didn't? If she could handle John, she could handle anything.

* * * * *

Take 4 Silhouette Desire novels
and a surprise gift
❧ FREE ❧

Then preview 6 brand-new Silhouette Desire novels—delivered to your door as soon as they come off the presses! If you decide to keep them, you pay just $2.24 each*—a 10% saving off the retail price, *with no additional charges for postage and handling!*

Silhouette Desire novels are not for everyone. They are written especially for the woman who wants a more satisfying, more deeply involving reading experience. Silhouette Desire novels take you beyond the others.

Start with 4 Silhouette Desire novels and a surprise gift absolutely FREE. They're yours to keep without obligation. You can always return a shipment and cancel at any time.

Simply fill out and return the coupon today!

*$2.25 each plus 69¢ postage and handling per shipment in Canada.

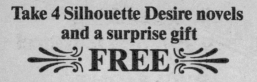

Silhouette ♥ Desire®

Clip and mail to: Silhouette Books

In U.S.:	In Canada:
901 Fuhrmann Blvd.	**P.O. Box 609**
P.O. Box 9013	**Fort Erie, Ontario**
Buffalo, NY 14240-9013	**L2A 5X3**

YES! Please rush me 4 free Silhouette Desire novels and my free surprise gift. Then send me 6 Silhouette Desire novels to preview each month as soon as they come off the presses. Bill me at the low price of $2.24 each*—a 10% saving off the retail price. There is no minimum number of books I must purchase. I can always return a shipment and cancel at any time. Even if I never buy another book from Silhouette Desire, the 4 free novels and surprise gift are mine to keep forever.

*$2.25 each plus 69¢ postage and handling per shipment in Canada.

225 BPY BP7F

Name _____ (please print)

Address _____ Apt. _____

City _____ State/Prov. _____ Zip/Postal Code _____

This offer is limited to one order per household and not valid to present subscribers. Price is subject to change.   D-SUB-1B

COMING NEXT MONTH

#205 ALL IN THE FAMILY— Heather Graham Pozzessere

Dan's daughter was going to have a baby, and Kelly's son was responsible. The children were happy, excited and in love, but Kelly and Dan were furious. Their fighting lasted until they realized just how close anger is to passion—and to love.

#206 GAUNTLET RUN—Robin Elliott

Hollis had come home to Texas to take over her father's ranch, but someone was trying very hard to chase her away. Cutter McKenzie had the ruthlessness to hurt her, but her heart wanted to believe that he never would.

#207 PASSAGE TO ZAPHIR—Anna James

Jenna Chapman needed a guide through Africa to help her discover the truth about her father's death, and Sam Matlock was just the man. Together they could risk any danger—even the danger of falling in love.

#208 ASKING FOR TROUBLE—Barbara Faith

Juliana Thornton was a rebel from way back, and Brian McNeeley had always represented the establishment to her. Then they met again on a dangerous tropical island and discovered that love knew no boundaries.

AVAILABLE THIS MONTH:

#201 HEARTBREAKER
Linda Howard

#202 PAST PERFECT
Sandy Steen

#203 CLOSE ENCOUNTER
Susanna Christie

#204 DANGER ZONE
Doreen Owens Malek